Praise for David

PROMISES

"A right rollickin' read, pardners. A roller-coaster, all-action, rootin'-tootin' ride, all the way from the cattle plains of Texas to the green, green grass of East Lotian. 'Promises' is what might properly be called a hoot. It's a love story, a tribute to Robert Burns. . . . a tear-jerker and an adventure all rolled up into one. . . . all told with a sort of irresistible American innocence and verve. . . . A heartwarming film is undoubtedly in the offing."
—*Catherine Lockerbie, The Scotsman, Book Reviews*

"I couldn't put the book, 'Promises,' down. It was absolutely the best story I have read in a long, long time. The author connected with both my wife and myself, so much so, that I told him that I'd love to play the lead role of 'Cappy' when it gets made into a movie. Keep your eye on this one."
—*Dennis Weaver, Hollywood Television Screen Actor*

"I read this novella months ago in its first draft and was captivated by the originality of its storyline by author-newcomer David Martin Anderson. Unique, emotional, and very, very moving!"
—*Hilly Elkins, Screen Agent*

"I can't wait to share this with my grandchildren. . . ."
—*Barbara Bush*

"Paula and I read this book and fell in love with it. It's a wonderful story of family togetherness vividly told by an inspiring writer."
—*Jim Coburn, Oscar Winning Hollywood Screen A*ctor

"I just read the book and enjoyed it immensely and found it interesting."
—*Larry Hagman, Majlar Productions Corp.,*
   Hollywood Television Screen Actor

"I read this book last night and just couldn't put it down. The rich family relationships are so visual and full that you really feel you know these people and are feeling with them and for them. If you love animals and talk to them, as I do, you will really relate to Cappy's 'heart to heart' with his herd, his 'children.' I have horses and dogs and tell them my inner most thoughts. . . . and they listen and understand. Pass this book on to your friends. It's a keeper."
—*Alice Billings, Independence Net*

". . .I especially liked the parts about our beautiful Texas wildflowers."
—*Lady Bird Johnson*

"I'm not particularly fond of romantic-style fiction but this book was so unique, I made an exception. I loved how the family pulled together to overcome 'the odds' against them. It was very moving and I think we'll see this as a classic motion picture someday."
— *Cowboy Larry Bonnville*

David Martin Anderson

* * * * *

Promises

a novella

ConRoca Publishing

ConRoca Publishing
132 Ridge Trail
Boerne, TX 78006
210.485.6764

Visit our website at
http://www.conrocapublishing.com

Author contact: davidmartinanderson@hotmail.com

ISBN 978-1-892617-22-4 (Paperback)
ISBN 978-1-892617-23-1 (Digital)

Printed in the United States of America - 2012

10 9 8 7 6 5 4 3 2 1

To Texas, Scotland, and My Miss Mary

Foreword

This book has history. Written as a novella in 1998 under the title *The Cowboys of Haddington Moor*, it was my second attempt at writing and a somewhat awkward attempt at that. Nevertheless, given the misspellings, gaffs, atrocious sentence structures and lack of editorial acumen (I'd like to think I've gotten better at the craft over the years), readers were surprisingly swept away by the story, itself—it seemed to possess something captivating. Thus, I have attempted to improve upon it with this latest version.

Back in 1998, and within days of receiving my first cache of books from the printer, I began mailing copies to reviewers, newspapers, and bookstore buyers. I also pitched the book to ten actors whom I felt could favorably portray a lead role should the book ever get made into a movie. Within weeks, I heard back from most of those actors including Charlton Heston and Larry Hagman. I also heard from James Coburn and Dennis Weaver who immediately began competing against each other for the film rights (Jim won). Both actors wanted to play the lead role of 'Cappy.' Both saw a film version as their swan song performance. Unfortunately, Jim passed away before he and his agent, Hilly Elkins, could ever see his dream materialize. Dennis passed away a few years later.

My wife, Mary, and I were fortunate to have spent New Year's Eve with Jim and Paula Coburn at their residence in Beverly Hills in 2000, ten months after Jim won an Academy Award for Best Supporting Actor. At that party, we met some of Jim's closest Hollywood friends. All were extraordinarily gracious and kind. In fact, when I arrived at Jim's home, most of them had already read the book and knew me, an unknown-but-aspiring author. *Go figure*! Ever since that event, Jim and his friends have remained golden in my memories.

Of the dozen or so books I have since written, this one by far has the most heart. At its core is a love story, but to classify it merely a romance would be misleading. It is also a family saga and, perhaps, a modern-day Western. And, for all the reasons already noted, I decided to re-write it and re-title it. The book simply needed a fresh start and was too good to languish unheralded and forgotten. I hope I have done *Promises* justice. If you enjoy it, please tell your friends and family. I can certainly use your help in spreading the word. Much appreciated.

Some books are lies from end to end,
And some great lies were never penn'd:
Even Ministers they have been known,
In holy rapture,
A rousing word, at times, to vend,
And nail 't wi' Scripture.

But this that I am gaun to tell,
Which lately in a night befell,
Is just as true as the Devil in hell,
or Dublin City. . . .

Robert Burns
from *Death and Dr. Hornbrook*

PROLOGUE

As a teen, I loved listening to my grandparents' stories, particularly the recollection about their chance encounter in London during the Second World War. Prior to 1943, Grandfather had never ventured outside of Texas. Such was the plight of an only son needed to tend the family ranch. Hard work and surviving the dust bowl days of the Great Depression posed even greater restrictions. "I rarely went without food," he once told me, "but always hungered for a new pair of boots." Wedging cardboard cutouts inside the bottoms of his battered shoes became an everyday occurrence in those impoverished days. It was a fortuitous set of events, however, that eventually took him from poverty to the engineering school at the University of Texas. From there he went to Great Britain, courtesy of the Army Air Corps, where he discovered Grandmother in the underground tubes while seeking shelter from V1 buzz bombs.

Grandmother never experienced material trappings, either. Tenth generation farmers in Scotland in the 1930s knew more about breeding cattle than breeding shillings, according to Grandmother. After turning sixteen, she was booted out the door and whisked to finishing school in London, this being her mother's attempt to exorcise "tomboyish mannerisms unbefitting a young lady." And, although Grandmother dearly missed the old farm, she always knew that someday she would return to her birthright with or without her mother's permission.

In her days as a youth, Grandmother earned the

equivalent of ten cents a week doing chores—shoveling manure, emptying feedbags, and inoculating heifers—the sort of work considered more like play than drudgery in Grandmother's eyes. In turn, the allowance got secretly stashed and hoarded under a bedroom floorboard for passage to America, a deep-rooted passion of hers flamed by the local movie house.

As the story goes, Grandmother would steal away on Saturday afternoons to swoon to the likes of Gene Autry and Tom Mix. As a matter of routine, her brother, James, would be dispatched to summon her return but, like most ultimatums, she would refuse to leave until the show finished. Later, she would pay the price for stubbornness with a welcome-home thrashing. Punishment never mattered to Grandmother for even at age eleven her headstrong conviction defied pre-adolescent logic. You see, sometime during the summer of 1936 she had a premonition of venturing to America and becoming a cattle baroness. Later in life, she stated coming to Texas fulfilled the premonition but marrying Grandfather made all her dreams come true.

From those Saturday matinees, Grandmother memorized the best celluloid virtues America offered the world—of honesty, hard work, commitment, and good always triumphing over evil. Perhaps that is why she insisted my older cousin and I recite *The Cowboy Oath* so often. "A cowboy always keeps his word," we would chant over and over with our hands pressed flat against our hearts. Eventually, I, too, became a believer in the old ways, especially the importance of fulfilling a promise.

The story you are about to read transpired when I was a younger man. It is a tale about a wonderful heritage known within our family circle as Haddington Moor, about traditions passed from one generation to another, and, most importantly, about keeping one's word.

Discoveries

Life is but a day at most,
Sprung from night, in darkness lost;
Hope not sunshine every hour,
Fear not clouds will always lour.

Robert Burns

ONE

(1996)

The road north from San Angelo traveled straight and true. It had been driven countless times before. What normally prompted the excursions included both the weekly grocery shopping at the only H-E-B for two hundred miles and the impulse purchases at the local quick-mart located halfway between the ranch and the small metropolis. On this particular day, however, there was a third item on the agenda. As she gripped the steering wheel of the old jalopy, her hands trembled. A follow-up visit to the doctor preempted today's routine and the news was not good. . . .

"Mary Catherine, please—*please have a seat*," her doctor pleaded while gesturing to a chromed armchair in the examining room.

"No," she replied straight-out. Whatever he needed to say she would endure standing. She was born a MacLaren and the MacLaren clan always took news flat on their feet and looking fate square in the eye. Life, she reminded him, was nothing more than a day at most, all sprung from night and all in the hands of the Maker. How bad could the test results possibly be? Even so, her body shivered as damp air from the swamp cooler wetted her frail shoulders. Why do doctors keep their offices so frightfully cold? she wondered, forgetting for an instant the reason for the follow-up.

The doctor struggled with his own set of feelings. For a few seconds he studied the floor and fretted with the stethoscope dangling about his neck. Thoughts of how best to divulge the truth made for a long awkward silence. Before him stood a familiar face washed by years of sun and wind and dust; it was a face tested by weeks of worry and months of illness that somehow seemed unfazed by the dire circumstances. In a way, he expected as much.

He had always been astonished by her ability to defy nature and rise above life's insurmountable odds. Even in the summers as a teen, in the late 1960's when he worked her ranch, he discovered she possessed a steadfast conviction more seasoned ranchers never attained. It was as though she had achieved a Zen-like understanding of why God planted her on this sweet earth. Being at peace, she always wore a resolute countenance.

Moreover, he shared a common history with her family. He grew up with her two sons. He birthed the grandsons and set the leg twice on her cowboy. Unfortunately, he knew her all too well and nothing could have ever prepared him for this. Today the odds got stacked cruelly against her and there would be no defying God. He looked away and swallowed hard. Then, *he* sat in the chrome armchair and gathered her hands in his.

"Mary Catherine, I'm afraid the biopsy turned out positive again. Everything indicates the disease has spread far beyond any conventional treatments we can give you here in San Angelo."

"How long do I have?" she asked. Avoiding the doctor's

face, she turned slightly to gaze past the window and watch a cardinal basking in the sunlight on a sycamore limb.

"Maybe a few months. The pills will help—"

"*No.* No pills, Billy. Thank you very much, but no pills. What little time I have left, I want to be coherent. I want to enjoy my family. I want dignity in death."

The doctor stood to embrace her and brush back a tear smudging the makeup on her cheek but she refused his gesture. Once again, her strength moved him.

"Well, Billy, I guess—I guess I best be goin' home. Cappy and the boys will be expecting their supper on time. Today is the end of the roundup. If it's to be the last time I get to watch my cowboys bring home the cattle, I want to be there."

"Have you told Cappy about the cancer?" the doctor asked.

"No, but I will. I will when the time is right."

. . .With those words still fresh on her mind, the sixty-mile drive home along Highway 87 meant even more to her that April afternoon. In spite of fifty-one years of living in a land akin to an arid savannah, she had never grown tired of the scenery. Today, the countryside rejoiced in springtime revelry just for her. The prickly pears danced in full bloom, carpeting the horizon with yellow blossoms in a frenzied display. Their temperamental petals would only last a few days but in their brief lifespan reign supreme over the parched plateau flats. The other wildflowers, particularly the bluebonnets and Indian paintbrushes, also cast a special brilliance. Adorning the road's broad shoulders, they would endure longer than their succulent cousins and inherit the sunshine for weeks to follow.

She smiled at the delicate creations as they swept by her open window. Over the years, she had fallen hopelessly in love with the flowers and this strange place called Texas.

This land stood in stark contrast to the manicured green of her native Scotland.

And, like the year before and the year before that, she marveled at how such frail flowers survived such harsh elements. So contrary to the natural order of things, she reminded herself. "Why, if a wildflower can survive West Texas, I, too, should be able to last a wee bit longer," she whispered, reassuring herself there was still time to blossom.

All too soon, the quick-mart crept in sight. She double-clutched the Land Rover Defender into third gear and then, into second to avoid wearing its temperamental brakes. The jalopy ground to a slower speed and coasted to a stop where she always parked—the location marked 'Expectant Mothers and Handicapped.'

"Not bad. Not bad at all," she remarked aloud. "For a sick lassie of seventy-two, you're still pretty darned good behind the wheel of *Old Rover*."

She adored the jalopy. Her father purchased it back in 1953. When he died fifteen years later, he bequeathed his prized possession to her. Just getting Old Rover shipped from Edinburgh to Texas stood a remarkable feat. Getting the US Customs Office to relinquish it from the docks of Houston posed an even greater challenge. She couldn't help but recall how Cappy fought the government over the vehicle, all because he made a promise to bring it back to the ranch in one piece, the way her father had intended. . . .

"It doesn't meet our new Federal air pollution guidelines, sir," the inspector told Cappy. "It's just that simple. The Port of Houston can not release the vehicle unless you're willing to remove the engine."

"The devil you say." Cappy balked, stopping short of strangling the civil servant. "It seems you don't understand my situation. I told my wife I'd drive her father's car back today come hell or high water. I made a promise and *I always keep my word.* Now, where's your boss, young man?"

"He's on vacation this week, sir, but I can assure you that his position and mine are unanimous—the car simply can't be released."

"Well, who other than you do I need to talk with to straighten this matter out?"

"That depends how far you intend to take the matter, sir."

"*How far*? As far as I have to," Cappy responded, thrusting himself within inches of the inspector's face.

"Well, sir, are you prepared to take the matter all the way to Jesus Christ, Himself, because that's who you're going to have to talk with to get an override out of me."

"Tell you what, sonny. I'm willing to take my fight all the way to Washington DC if that's where He lives."

Cappy had always been a stalwart proponent for keeping his word. Fortunately, *Jesus* lived in the form of a Houston district supervisor who was also a staunch University of Texas alum and who was willing to stretch the rules that day for an old friend.

. . .As Mary Catherine opened the door on the Defender, a hinge void of oil since 1968 groaned in pain. She ignored its agony and scooted herself sideways on the torn canvass seat, teetered over the seat's edge, and prepared to take the eighteen-inch plunge to the ground like an experienced paratrooper. Gripping the interior handle bar located above the door, the infamous *mackerel* bar, she couldn't help but recall the incident stirring the handle's nickname and the memory of the wild rides behind the wheel of Old Rover.

As a much younger woman, Mary Catherine's reputation as a thrill seeker often preceded her. Back in the late 1960s she delighted at driving, as Cappy so colorfully described, "like a bat out of hell" while taking dangerous windy curves as fast as possible. Hence, the much deserved title throughout the county: 'Tempest in the four-by-four'. . . .

"Now, Cappy, what are you so worried about? Flipping? That's what the exterior roll bars on Old Rover are for," she would happily tell him.

"Miss Mary, it's bad enough the steering wheel is on the wrong side of this contraption, but the roll bars—the roll bars are supposed to be there in the event of an accident, not in spite of you creating one."

However, they never did flip. Each time she would take a curve, he would grab the overhead handle bar, grip it for dear life and pray aloud so even she could hear his divine beseeching. "Dear Jesus: If You'll see me safely through this day in this piece of junk, I promise I will never curse, use Your name in vain, or look at other women."

The prayer did not set well with Mary Catherine.

"So, ya been lookin' at other women, have ya?" she chided, evoking her sternest brogue and throwing the Defender into a dusty one-eighty tailspin. Two things brought out the brogue in Mary Catherine—tequila and temper.

"Holy *Mackerel*," Cappy shrieked. "Are you trying to kill us? I was just teasing about the women." Instinctively, he clutched the overhead handle bar and hung on for dear life.

"Well, ya had better been a teasin' and that's all ya had better been doin' John David or it is *snip, snip*—if ya know what I mean." She flashed her two fingers in scissors-fashion, eyeing him below the belt.

After the incident, the interior handle bars, like the one Mary Catherine now gripped in her own hands, simply became known to them both as the *mackerel* bars.

. . .She grinned recalling those days from so long ago but, wasting scant time on memories, prepared herself to take the plunge from Old Rover. Within seconds, her feet plopped to the gravel with a solid thump. Turning around, she patted the vehicle's side door and whispered to it like a doting mother. "Father would be so proud of you, Old Rover. You've conquered Texas as victoriously as the moors."

Taking a dollar from her purse, she climbed the short staircase. Upon reaching the porch landing, the ascent proved too strenuous. She stumbled and leaned hard against the screen door for support and deliberately measured her lungs' efforts to consume air. In less than a minute, however, she had willed herself onward through the entrance and, soon enough, stood before a bleached Formica-topped counter and the youthful shopkeeper.

"Good afternoon, Mrs. Sterling. How are you this beautiful afternoon?" the voiced beamed.

"Oh, Lupe, how could anyone not relish a spring day like today and still call themselves part of the humanity of man? Or, rather, should I say the humanity of *wo*-man?"

"Well, I think it should be 'of woman.' After all, those men of ours would be lost without us. And, I wholeheartedly agree with you about relishing the day. It's absolutely gorgeous outside."

Lupe not only managed the isolated trading post disguised as a quick-mart convenience store, she was also the love-interest of Mary Catherine's adopted son, Emilio. After years of association, Lupe knew Wednesday afternoons, shopping day, were reserved for serious business—serious dog business.

"I've found the prettiest bandanna for Pedo. Look at this," Lupe said, unfolding a bright florescent-green neckerchief. "That dog of yours will be the best dressed blue heeler in the county."

Every Wednesday for the past seven years, Mary Catherine found time to adorn her cattle dog with a bandanna. She said it soothed the savage beast in him and made him more civilized.

"I think this one is positively outrageous, Lupe. He'll love it." Mary Catherine giggled, sounding more like a little girl than a matronly cattle baroness. She laid the cloth out on the countertop for better viewing. "It's so—so *MTVish*."

"Don't tell me you're still letting Pedo watch that channel off the satellite dish, Mrs. Sterling?"

"Well, if I don't let him, he whines and whimpers like a baby. He likes the rappers."

Lupe laughed loudly. She found Mary Catherine full of spunk.

"You know, Lupe, that today is the day our cowboys will be coming home," Mary Catherine continued. "Why don't you come by the ranch at 6:00PM to watch them drive in the cattle? I'm anticipating their arrival shortly thereafter. We'll have some hardy *English coffee* and ginger snaps as we wait. If the boys had a good roundup, they should be bringing in over two thousand head. Won't that be a sight? Let's keep our fingers crossed for good luck."

Once a year her cowboys rode west into the thicket of scrub and cactus on Rancho Rio Concho to retrieve the foraging cattle herd. The 30,640 acres of land was harsh and arid and rarely exhumed cattle without a wrestling. These days it took more than fifteen acres per head to sustain a single animal and with the cost of grain supplement skyrocketing, turning a profit had become an ambitious challenge. At one time the ranch hands numbered in the teens, but no more. Now they were down to six seasoned drovers: Cappy, Emilio, grandsons Nathaniel and Steven, an uncanny lead longhorn named Big Ben, and the animated blue heeler named Pedo.

"Mrs. Sterling, there's nothing I'd like better than to watch the boys bring the cattle over the crest of Little Concho Ridge. You've got a date."

"Oh, how wonderful, Lupe. It's such a magnificent sight. You'll see. You'll see." Mary Catherine giggled. With those words said, she unexpectedly turned and bolted out the front entrance with the screen door slamming behind her.

Seconds later, Lupe realized her friend had forgotten the other reason for the afternoon stop and ran after her. "Wait, Mrs. Sterling. You forgot the sunflower seeds for Sir Charles," she yelled through the screen door. But, the Defender was already racing down the highway with Mary Catherine absorbed in the day's events, the wildflowers, and thoughts of her cowboys.

Here's to thy health, my bonnie lassie,
Goodnight and joy be with thee;
I'll come no more to thy back door,
To tell thee that I love thee.

Robert Burns

TWO

The last leg of the drive home wrapped around familiar mesas and wind eroded hillsides, and eventually gave way to the semi-green of the Concho River valley. The seasonal tributary cut a diagonal swath through the ranch property. On one side lay Little Concho Ridge and the river, and on the other side, the ranch house and Highway 87. The rock dwelling, itself, encircled by row after row of wooden stockade used to separate and pen livestock. Like a citadel with timber fencing as a moat, their West Texas castle stood as grand as any in all of Scotland, Mary Catherine often proclaimed.

Reluctantly, the Land Rover came to a grinding halt in front of a wrought iron gate, and stopped short of the cattle grate that maintained civil obedience from Brangus foraging for territorial freedom. Mary Catherine parked next to a galvanized mailbox, rolled down the window and unlatched the lid. Reaching inside, she pulled out an assortment of mail including the junk mail that inevitably found its way to her oasis in the Llano Estacado. Sorting through multicolored envelopes and flyers, she found the one item that she had been waiting for, the monthly letter from her brother, James. She hurriedly tore open the envelope and spread out the single page of correspondence.

April 15, 1996

My Bonnie Mary Catherine,

I apologize for the brevity of this letter, dear sister. I know how much you look forward to hearing from me but things have been a bit hectic lately at Haddington Moor. Last weekend Angus had to euthanize our few remaining head of cattle due to the 'mad cow' epidemic that has so ravaged the Lowlands. Many of the surrounding farms have had to capitulate to the bank. I'm afraid, dear sister, that even though we've made good on our loan, the bank will call the note if we can't show we've got an ongoing cattle production facility, and with the government's proposed embargo on imported breeders, it may mean the end of our family's land. I feel so bad in asking you this but if there is any way that you and Cappy can help us out, our family and our ancestors would be greatly obliged. Give my best to your cowboy for me.

Love, as always, springs from the heather and rye of Haddington Moor.

Your brother,
James

She sighed before slowly folding and pleating the letter, and placed it back inside the envelope. She knew with her illness that she and Cappy could never provide financial assistance. A tear welled in her eyes. It had not been a good day, she told herself. In fact, it had been the worst of days. Memories of Haddington Moor, however, always brought her peace of mind and, like on so many other occasions when she became homesick or worried, she reminisced about the farm tucked in the heart of the Lothians of Scotland. Even though she had not been home for over fifty years, she could still picture the hills, experience the smell of the wild pink twinflowers, and feel the grassy fields under her feet. She could still dream of her birthright as though it was only yesterday. She closed her eyes and chanted the words, "Haddington Moor. Haddington Moor. Haddington Moor." Within seconds, the mantra whisked her imagination five thousand miles away beyond the vast tract of ocean and the Lammermoor Hills, and through the Lothian valleys and the rolling meadows with their endless flowers and rock wall hedges. The green of her secret lookout was the place she once claimed as her own as a child; it would always remain in her heart and a part of her soul. She had never forgotten the family's green parcel that now belonged to her and James and the kin. How could she? Haddington Moor breathed of life—her life.

The relentless rapping, pecking to be exact, interrupted Mary Catherine's transcendental pilgrimage. An annoying roadrunner had attached itself to Old Rover's wiper blades and roosted in earnest attacking the windshield.

"My goodness, Sir Charles. You gave me such a startle. Shame on you, you bad, bad boy."

Emptying the contents of an already opened sunflower packet into a hand, she wrapped her arm around the windshield and held out a seed-laden palm.

The gangly bird eyed the morsels and cautiously hopped to its awaiting dinner treat. With head bobbing up and down, and eyeing underneath and above the open hand, the bird decided once again Mary Catherine and her treats were safe. After all, sunflower seeds were the stuff dreams were made of to *Sir Charles* the pet chaparral.

The half-mile drive from the highway wound its way into the horseshoe enclave of the ranch headquarters. Cottonwood trees, now in full bloom, surrounded the one-story washed rock house and provided a break from the perpetual winds out of the west. An eight-foot-wide wood porch girdled the shelter, protecting it from the harsh mid-afternoon sunlight. The back porch, however, is where Mary Catherine's senses would bask in the spectacle of the cattle drive coming to its conclusion. After years of cattle drives, she had grown to savor the sounds and the images of her cowboys' approach—the most breathtaking sensation being her Sterling men driving the herd over Little Concho Ridge. With a cloud of dust rising like steam about their shoulders, the fading sunset would melt into an orange glow spanning the horizon. The sounds of thunderous hoofs pounding the earth, the bawling of cattle pushed to their limits, and the drovers' shrill whistles would heighten the excitement. The spectacle recalled the American West she had fallen in love with as a child at the local movie theater on Saturday afternoons—an image that defied time at Rancho Rio Concho.

She entered the main house and immediately withdrew to the bedroom to change her clothes and look her best for Cappy. It was in the kitchen, however, where she spent the rest of the afternoon, preparing the feast for the famished cowboys. As the day progressed, she occasionally peeked out the kitchen window to measure the sun's position. Once it reached an angle directly above the horizon, she knew the time of approach was at hand.

Seizing a handful of ginger snaps from the cookie jar, she scattered the confections in a spiraled fashion on a silver tray and adorned the tray's edges with petite yellow and shell-colored wildflowers. Next, she placed a black clay bottle of Hussong tequila in the center of the tray and surrounded it with milk bone demitasse cups, china that once belonged to her mother.

"There, Mother," she exclaimed aloud when finished with the arrangement. "We're almost civilized, are we not?"

An unexpected voice from the back door answered.

"Are you home, Mrs. Sterling? It's me, Lupe. I thought I heard your voice in there. Are you okay?"

"Yes, dear." Mary Catherine moaned, knowing full well her deceased mother could never have answered the question. "Stay right there, Lupe. I have our hardy English coffee ready for the boys and us. Let me bring everything outside to you."

Lupe held the kitchen door open as Mary Catherine stepped over the threshold and onto the planked porch. Leading her friend to an outdoor wicker table, she laid the contents on top but right away began wheezing from the expended burst of energy.

"Are you sure you're all right, Mrs. Sterling?"

Mary Catherine soon regained enough composure to respond. "No problem, dear. I'm just a bit under the weather, that's all."

The two sat at the table and Mary Catherine encouraged her friend to face the west and the most probable line of the cattle drive approach. By now, the sun had sunk low on the horizon and the first glimpse of its departure could be seen. The sky had turned bright marmalade orange and promised to put on a more spectacular show as nighttime drew nearer.

"It is so beautiful here," Lupe stated.

"Just wait, dear. It gets even better," Mary Catherine replied, nodding her head as her finger pointed toward the ridge. "It gets much better."

After a few seconds, Lupe noticed the tray's contents with

its interlaced pattern of wildflowers and cookies and tequila. "Excuse me, Mrs. Sterling. You must have forgotten the coffee. Would you like me to go back inside and get it?"

"Coffee? Oh, that. You mean real coffee. No, dear, it's not necessary. When our cowboys come home, after a successful roundup, tequila becomes our *hardy English coffee*—just part of our tradition." She giggled, pouring a shot of tequila into one of the demitasse cups. "It's a tradition I'm sure Mother would never have approved."

Handing the cup to Lupe, Mary Catherine poured herself two fingers' worth of the potion in her own cup.

"There. Let's toast. What would you like me to toast, dear? Your choice."

"Well, I really don't know. I've never toasted anything before. How about to our cowboys, Mrs. Sterling?"

"Oh, that's a good choice, dear—one I will never ever grow tired of. You do know my weakness, don't you?"

Mary Catherine abruptly scooted back her chair and stood at attention facing Lupe so she could properly exalt the cowboys and declare her sentiments for the men she loved. Clearing her throat for oration, she spoke the cheer recited for many years but now shared with her young friend:

"Here's to our cowboys:

> May they live to ride for another day,
> with the wind always at their backs;
> May they never lose a head of steer,
> in the hostile Texas cracks;
> May they always shine in the Maker's eyes,
> as they ride tall upon the saddle,
> And may He guide their way for another day,
> to come hither through the rattle.

To their continued good fortune and health."

Lupe smiled and clanked her cup against the cup belonging to the matron of Rancho Rio Concho. Then, both heads snapped backward downing the Mexican elixir.

"I didn't know you were such a poet Mrs. Sterling," Lupe said, patting her lips dry.

"Aye. That I am but not nearly like Cappy. He loves Robert Burns, you know. I think that's one of the reasons I fell so madly in love with him. When he knows I'm in a homesick blue mood for Scotland, he reads me the melancholy verses from the greatest poet of my native land."

"I did not know that. Know what else? I think I just detected a hint of Scottish accent."

"Aye. I'm sure you did. The more I drink, the clearer the br-r-rogue." Mary Catherine winked, clanging her cup against Lupe's for a second time and slurping the remains of the tequila. "You can take the girl out of Scotland but you can never take Scotland out of the girl."

Lupe laughed and grabbed Mary Catherine's hand, encouraging her to sit back down. "Mrs. Sterling, you are a hoot. Now I know why Emilio loves you so much."

"Ah-h-h-h, and we love him too, dear, as though he is our very own. When his mother died, he was only nine years old. Cappy was so heartbroken over the loss. She had worked for us for years and was like one of the family. One day out of the clear, he says to me, 'Miss Mary, the boy's a natural with the whip and loves it here. Can we keep him?' Well, I laughed and said, 'Cappy, he's not a lost puppy you can make into a pet. He's a child for goodness sake. But, yes, I would like that very much, too.' That was fourteen years ago, Lupe, and I wouldn't trade all the tea in China for our son. Our wonderful Tejano cowboy."

As Mary Catherine talked, Lupe poured another round of tequila.

"I'll drink to Emilio, Mrs. Sterling," Lupe chortled, raising her cup and making a hand gesture toward the grand dame.

"Please—please, call me Mary or Mary Catherine."

"Not Miss Mary?"

"Heavens, no. That's a man's thing. Between us lassies informality is what counts. After all, are we not the unpretentious gender of the sexes? Especially out here at the ranch? It seems to me. . . ."

As Mary Catherine continued to speak, the empty demitasse cups suddenly began to rattle and vibrate off the tray. Lupe placed her hands on the tray to keep its contents from falling off the table.

"What in the world is going on? Are we having an earthquake, Mary Catherine?"

"Aye. One made by man and beast. Our cowboys are coming home, dear Lupe. They're coming home."

Soon the quaking ceased, only to be replaced by a low-pitched growl. As if on cue, the two women stood with their hands shielding their eyes from the direct rays of the setting sun, and peered westward to the ridge a half-mile away. The sound of thundering hoofs crescendoed like a freight train's approach and began echoing off the rocky incline leading from the riverbank. As the rumble grew, dust exploded skyward until the sun's rays blotted dark amber from refraction, and a lone bull magically appeared on the crest's shoulders. The bull bowed at the sight of the ranch enclave and carved the ground with a front hoof as though ready to charge at the stockades.

"My God, is that your longhorn, Big Ben? He's so—so magnificent."

"Aye. He's the lead bull. The rest will be following shortly. You'll see."

As soon as she spoke those words, Brangus bulls, nearly one hundred strong, lumbered from behind following Big Ben's lead. Next rushed the mismashed assortment of Aberdeen Angus steers, Galloway heifers, calves, and Pedo the dog. Driving the cattle from the rear and funneling the contingent from both sides rode the four Sterlings. Waving their arms in the air, hats slapping the hindquarters of their

horses' flanks, whistling and shouting, the cowboys pushed
the last of the stragglers forward. Emilio's whip cracked the
air with a sonic concussion, startling the most timid of the
beasts. And, the arid land seemed to split wide open by the
frenzy of the procession and the reunion weeks in the
making.

Mary Catherine watched the sun play with the illuminated
images of her cowboys. Each glowed from behind in a fired
aureole of light close about their silhouettes.

"They look like angels to me, Lupe," she said. "So much
like angels."

As the herd stampeded toward the river, the cowboys
could make out two distant specters through the dust cloud;
both figures locked in a frozen trance at the ranch house
porch. The eldest cowboy spotted Mary Catherine and bolted
down the incline, whacking his steed's shoulders with the
reins to gallop within earshot. His palomino knew the routine
all too well and tossed its head sideways in showy triumph.
Suddenly, the horse braked and craned vertical, its front
hoofs jabbing an invisible foe as his master waved a Stetson
high through the amber. From afar, Cappy hailed, "You're
looking beautiful as ever, Miss Mary."

She raised her cup in reciprocal signaled fashion where he
could see it. A tear splashed on the shoulders of her chiffon
dress. She adored her cowboys, especially her hero, Cappy.
Nevertheless, the cow dog stole the moment. Leaping upon
one of the vacant wicker chairs, Pedo jiggled the table. One
of the cups fell crashing into pieces on the planks. As if
embarrassed by the awkward show of excitement, the dog
whimpered and buried its head under its paws.

"Well, well, well. You just made a bit of a fool of yerself
again, didn't ya?" Mary Catherine scolded.

Pedo muffled two yelps.

"So, I bet ya think I've got something for ya, aye?"

With the dog's tail now furiously fanning the air, Mary

Catherine could no longer hide what concealed in a pocket. When she pulled out the florescent green bandanna, Pedo barked in jubilation over his new apparel; his earlier transgression was forgotten as easily as the china pieces that fell between cracks in the planks.

"Here ya go, but don't tell the others where ya got it—especially Cappy," she said, folding the cloth in a triangular wedge and knotting it around Pedo's thick neck. "He doesn't know that we're in love," Mary Catherine added in a whisper.

Lupe laughed at the admission.

"Now, here's a ginger snap for ya and one for Big Ben," Mary Catherine continued, making sure Pedo had consumed the treat before handing over the second for the longhorn. "Off ya go. And be a good boy."

The blue heeler gummed the cookie, jumped off the chair, and dashed toward the privileged straw-lined compound of Ben the bull.

"Now, Mary Catherine, do you really think Pedo is going to give that ginger snap to Ben?" Lupe asked skeptically.

"Dear, he'd better or I will personally kick him in the rump. Here, have another shot of tequila."

With that said, the two women decided it best to continue toasting—to their men, to Texas and Scotland, and to whatever else struck their fancy.

It took an hour for the last of the cattle to cross the shallow river. One by one, they were culled into the cross-sectioned stockyard. By 9:00PM, the hard-heeled boots and clanging spurs of the men pounded the planks leading to the kitchen threshold. Mary Catherine opened the door long before anyone could rap the window. Gazing up into her husband's eyes, at seventy-eight year's young, John David Sterling still struck a handsome pose. Upon seeing Mary Catherine in the doorway, Cappy smiled and politely removed his hat. A tuft of thin gray hair tumbled over his eyes. She wet her thumb and index finger with saliva, creased the dangling strands, and pushed the hair back in place. Within seconds her efforts to correct the cowlick failed as the tuft collapsed once again.

"That never does work, Miss Mary."

"Well, Cappy, you can't stop a girl from trying to tame the wild things."

Leaning over her so not to spoil the chiffon dress with his dust encrusted shirt and leather chaps, he kissed her on the cheek.

"I missed you," he whispered. "Shoot, we all missed you."

She smiled softly up at him. "The nights were very lonely here without you, my sweet husband."

Little Nate unexpectedly interrupted the tender exchange by bursting past Cappy and grabbing hold of Mary Catherine in his arms. He swung his grandmother around in circles, nearly upsetting the kitchen chairs and the neatly stacked countertops. Dust flew through the air with most of it sticking to her dress.

"Grandma, I missed you worse than that old buzzard." Nate teased.

"Nathaniel, stop it. Stop this nonsense immediately," she shrieked, attempting to restore whatever decorum remained of the moment. "Where are your manners, young man? Your respectability?"

"Heck, Grandma. I believe my manners is all over the front of your dress." He smirked. "And here comes respectability." His thumbs and index fingers suddenly began pinching in the crab-like motion she abhorred.

"No, Nathaniel. No pinching. You cannot pinch your grandmother. It is forbidden by order of the house. No, pinching," she threatened while attempting to hide a gleeful half-smile and fight off the effects of tequila.

The seventeen-year-old loved to tease his grandmother. No one would have ever suspected that a year earlier he had been spiraling out of control using illegal drugs and an insolent attitude. His affluent lawyer-father had shipped him off to live with his grandparents. Austin had too many distractions, his father had said. Justifiably, it was the father's hope that life on the ranch would exorcise the boy's demons. Through it all, Nathaniel Robert Sterling had made a miraculous comeback. He loved the cowboy ways and cherished his grandparents who only saw the good inside him.

"Grandma, I hope you didn't give that dog of yours ginger snaps. You know how it makes him fart something fierce," Nate continued ranting.

"Well, first Nathaniel, we don't ever use that word in this house. You may use the phrase 'pass gas', or 'pass wind,' or the Mex-Tex equivalent which is—"

"*Pedo*. I know, Grandma, I know. Pedo, the farting dog." He belly-laughed.

Steven winced. Four weeks in the wilds with his hyperactive attention deficit cousin had pushed the limits of his patience. Steven, the more serious of the two grandsons, had dedicated himself to the profession of cattle ranching after laboring four years at Texas A&M to become even more proficient in the family business. Nate's perpetual antics, however, had worn him thin—irritatingly thin. He whispered, not so quietly to his grandfather, "Little Nate's out of control, again. You'd better make him take his medicine."

"Ah, it's nothing. He's just teasing his grandma. That's all." Nevertheless, watching Nate's non-stop antics, Cappy managed to whisper back, "Well, maybe you ought to see if you can distract him."

Steven seized the opportunity. "Take it easy on Grandma, little cousin. You're dealing with a feisty Scottish rose. Best be careful."

"Aye. I may be seventy-two but I can still put ya across me knee and give ya a good br-r-rashing," Mary Catherine slurred.

"You wouldn't dare 'brash' me, Grandma, cause I'm your favorite," Nate spouted back, flashing a wink.

"Indeed. I do believe you are the *brashest* one in the room," she replied, chuckling at her play on words.

"Little Nate, why don't you tell Grandma and Lupe about how Big Ben saved the day?" Steven coaxed.

Nate wasted no time. He loved being the center of attention. Telling yarns clearly put him in the spotlight. Now all eyes affixed on him, just the way he liked:

"It was like this: There we were driving over two thousand head down the Upper Concho. That darn wash was all dried up so we thought we'd use the gorge to avoid the rocky hills. Well now, the further we got into the gorge, the narrower and narrower it became. Finally got to a point where it was no wider than thirty-feet and no way out except moving forward or backward cause the bank was too steep to climb out of. So, we're pushing the herd fast and hard when Steven yells back to Grandpa, 'Turn 'em around. Turn 'em around *fellas*.'" Nate mocked Steven, flashing a limp wrist and impersonating an effeminate cowboy. Everyone laughed—except Steven. "You see, a big ole' cottonwood had fallen smack dab over and blocked our way. Darned thing must have been four-feet in diameter. Well, with nowhere else to go, the cattle panicked and Steven was in the thick of it all. It scared me to death. I thought he was a goner. That he'd get stampeded. Well, I yelled down to that dog of yours, 'Pedo, go get Big Ben and make him jump that tree.' And guess what? Pedo obeyed me. He bit and clawed his way to the front of the herd, fighting off those bulls, and he begins barking some gibberish at Ben and that son of a gun bull leaps over the cottonwood. The Brangus, they followed

Ben. And those heifers, they go wherever the bulls go. And then, Steven, Emilio, and I helped the calves over. Grandma, I'm telling you it was a sight I'll never forget. Big Ben's a dadgum jumper. I've heard of jumping longhorns but never thought I'd see the day."

Steven was still fuming from Nate's earlier wisecrack. He stepped up to Nate poking him in the chest. "Hey, I never act like a faggot."

"Oh, no, Aggie-boy? Seems to me by the end of the drive you were getting awful friendly with those purdy heifers. Too bad we didn't have sheep along on the drive," Nate replied, flashing another limp wrist and baaing like a lamb.

"Listen you little freak, if you hadn't been so strung out on drugs, you wouldn't be here in the first place and I wouldn't have to listen to your crap all day. You're just lucky Grandma let you stay."

Nate shoved Steven back. Steven drew a fist ready to fight but Cappy stepped in between the feuding cousins.

"Enough of this, you two. I'm tired of this constant bickering. Steven, you're the oldest. You know better. Little Nate is just teasing you. Get over it. And you," he turned to the youngest grandson, "you need to calm down. One of these days you're going to get your nose broke if you don't watch your mouth."

Nate knew exactly what his grandfather was attempting to do—calm him down and defuse the situation. Without forethought, he threw his arms around Cappy and buried his head into the elder's chest. "I'm real sorry, Grandpa. Sometimes I get a little crazy. Maybe it's because I don't know what I want out of life. I just keep wondering what's going happen to me. That's all."

While the two men embraced, Nate fingered Steven. No one else saw the gesture except the older cousin.

"Only good things are going to happen to you, Little Nate. Only good things. Just follow your heart. You'll see," Cappy assured.

Next, Steven took the floor.

"And Grandma, guess who met us yesterday on the drive?"

"Well, if history repeats itself, I'd say it would have to be that rascal of a neighbor, Zack Higginbotham."

"Yup. True to form. He camped out with us again last night like he has on the last three drives. He brought his *Cuervo* and tried to get Grandpa drunk so we'd sell the ranch to him. You'd think he'd be content with his 26,000-acre spread but no, ma'am. He's got to have the largest ranch in the county. It's a penis envy thing, Grandma. That's all it is."

"Well, Steven, in Scotland we have a saying that applies very appropriately to Mr. Higginbotham. It goes like this: The smaller the man's penis, the bigger his head."

Cappy turned red-faced and yanked Mary Catherine by the arm and toward the dining room. He spouted to the group, "Instead of standing here shooting the breeze, let's move out of the kitchen and start the ceremony. Lupe, go grab that boyfriend of yours and tell him to get in here pronto."

They marched into the adjoining room with Cappy forcibly dragging Mary Catherine. Steven smacked Nate on the side of the head with his cowboy hat when no one was looking, and threatened to do more serious damage if the teasing continued. Cappy lit a single white candle and placed it near the center of the dining table. He poured tequila in each of their demitasse cups. Once Emilio and Lupe had joined in, he positioned Mary Catherine at the head of the table in front of the fireplace. He assumed his position at the other end with Nate and Steven on his right, Emilio and Lupe on his left. Pedo, as always, affixed himself near his mistress. Finally, when all had been readied, Cappy addressed the worn cadre, repeating the speech they had grown to love.

"Gentlemen, Lupe, and Miss Mary: Years ago I made two promises to this wonderful lady you see before us. I haven't done too well with one of the promises, 'least not yet, but I've faithfully kept the other, which is the tradition we are about to celebrate here tonight. Now, the first promise I made was to toast Mary Catherine MacLaren Sterling whenever we succeeded in defying life's odds. Today we have all done that, for each time we bring home the cattle we defy both time and nature. With each successful roundup, we rise above our mere mortality and say to God, 'Look at me, for I am a king today. I have risen above the rattle.' Tonight, I salute the woman who has helped me defy the odds for all these years. So, everyone raise your glasses on high, and I hope Mr. Robert Burns, wherever you are or you're fixing to be, you'll forgive me again for butchering your poetry."

Cappy paused to gaze upon Mary Catherine. Somehow, she looked different tonight, he thought. Perhaps after fifty-one years she had finally grown weary of West Texas. Perhaps it was nothing at all. Then, he lifted his demitasse high in the air, cleared his throat, and recited the toast memorized as a much younger man:

"Go fetch to me a pint of wine,
and fill it in a *demitasse*;
That I may drink before I go,
a service to my bonnie lassie;
The boat rocks at the Pier of Leith,
full loud the wind blows from the ferry,
The ship rides by the Berwick Law,
that I may toast my bonnie Mary.

Gentlemen: To Texas, Scotland, and Miss Mary."

In unison, the cowboys responded: "TO TEXAS, SCOTLAND, AND MISS MARY."

She, too, remembered the two promises he had made in exchange for her hand in marriage. She swallowed hard on the tequila, trying to hold back tears. Looking at him smiling at her, she realized this would be their last toast together. She closed her eyes and thought back to the first time, to the very first toast so many years before. She loved the men in her life so very much, she thought, but she especially loved her cowboy.

Will ye go to the Indies, my Mary,
And leave old Scotland's shore;
Will ye go the Indies, my Mary,
Across the Atlantic roar.

Robert Burns

THREE

(1944)

The air raid siren wailed its familiar omen, warning the townspeople of London to take shelter from the approaching V1 rocket attack. A young woman scurried toward the safety of the Tube, the underground subway linking the city's inhabitants with the outlying areas. King's Cross Station stood only a short distance away. She knew at a moment's notice she could board one of the great steam locomotives running the northern route and return to Haddington Moor, but her mother had sent her south beyond the Borders to be educated and rid of her tomboyish ways. Until she could display "manners and respectability befitting a lady," she could not go home.

"Mary Catherine, it's just not r-r-right, ye working the fields with yer younger br-r-rother. It's a man's work, lassie, not fittin' for the likes of a lovely young lady like yerself," her mother lectured. "It's simply no good for the MacLaren clan. One of these days we got to marry ye off and ye got to be able to attract a man of means. Dressin' and talkin' like a man aren't going do it neither. So, it's off to school where they'll teach ye to speak in the proper tongue and train ye in manners and such."

Mary Catherine hated those words and resented the day her mother sent her south to London. She longed for the serenity of Haddington Moor and her secret place high on the hill. Looking to her left stood King's Cross. To her right hid a subway entrance. Fate was steering her decision that summer day of 1944 as much as the hesitancy to face a stern mother. As the sirens echoed down the proper dignified shops along Pentonville Road, Mary Catherine reluctantly chose the Tube.

Scurrying down an endless flight of concrete and tiled stairs, the deafening echo of sirens abated to the quiet hush of the tunnel. The others who had also flocked to the sanctity of the shelter were exchanging small talk. Mary Catherine leaned up against the white tiled wall alone and looked at her fellow humanity sharing what amounted to a subterranean lifeboat. They were all chattering and ignoring the buzz bombs ripping the buildings apart fifty feet above. Through the rumbling of the explosions and the violent vibrations shaking the foundations of the subway shelter, she could still hear their incessant conversations about the weather, about Mrs. Murphy's pregnant daughter, about the flowers at Primrose Garden, and about anything other than war. She also heard the two men talking in the corner. Both were aviators. One spoke in her native dialect. The other had a crude foreign familiarity. The foreigner appeared handsome in his Army Air Corps uniform and seemed so self-assured and gallant. She moved closer to eavesdrop on the conversation. "There," she whispered, jaw dropping in disbelief. "He said it again. He said, *fixing* in place of the word *going*."

Her curiosity got the best of her and with the sort of predictable, unabashed forwardness her mother hoped to un-cultivate, she tapped the tall stranger on the shoulder.

"Excuse me, kind sir. I don't mean to pry or appear too

forward, but by chance are you, or rather, I should say, before the war were you a cowboy?" She asked the question quite innocently and with only the best of intentions; her eyes trained on his for the highly anticipated response.

Taken aback and slightly bewildered by the young woman's assertive style, he said nothing but studied her face, thinking he had never seen anyone as beautiful. For the moment, he had become hopelessly tongue-tied.

"Captain Sterling is not only a cowboy, Miss, he's a r-r-rootin' tootin' pilot of eighteen missions above the land of the Hun," the man's Scottish friend remarked.

"Well, I—I couldn't help but overhear the two of you talking, and I detected what I thought was an impeccable Gene Autry sort of accent. You know, the actor-singer. I've always fancied him. Well, and, of course, Tom Mix, Smith Ballew, and my absolute favorite, the new one, Roy Rogers. I am the greatest of fans of the American Western epochs. Cowboys have been my heroes since I was a little girl. So, tell me, tall captain, from what state do you hail from?"

The pilot tipped his hat but the words remained locked in his mind with his mouth frozen shut.

"As you can see, lassie, the captain is a wee bit shy around our kind. R-r-robert Duffy's the name. May I have the honors to do the introduction?" He cleared his throat. "This fine specimen of cowboy Americana is none other than John David Sterling, one of the best B-17 pilots I've ever had the pleasure of flying with. And, I might add, he is from the great state of Texas. The land of the Alamo."

"*Texas*? Oh, how wonderful. How absolutely wonderful. Is it true, Captain Sterling, that the jackrabbits are as big as Irish setters in Texas, and to find oil all you have to do is dig three feet down into the ground? I've heard everyone chews tobacco and square dances themselves silly on Saturday nights. Do you play the guitar, Captain Sterling, while the doggies howl at the moon, and do you carry a six-shooter on your hip?" she joyously asked the questions, gazing up at him with her inquisitive eyes while thirsting for answers about the faraway places of America.

This time he carefully formulated his words. He had always been awkward around women and this one, he sensed, was special.

"I'm—I'm glad to see somebody has an interest in Texas as much as me. What's your name, Miss?"

"Mary. Mary Catherine MacLaren of Haddington Moor."

"Well, Miss, now that the sirens have stopped—" He hesitated. "Could you or, rather, would you like to accompany me and Duffy, here, for a cup of coffee or a spot of tea?"

"Why, I'd be honored, kind sir," she replied, thrusting an outstretched elbow so he couldn't help but interlock his arm with hers and escort her back up the staircase.

Wise Robert Duffy knew the two only had eyes for each other. "I believe I can't make this tea, Captain. Can I catch you two on the next outing?"

Turning to his bombardier, the captain leaned over and whispered in the man's ear, "I can't do this alone, Robert. You know how I am around women."

The seasoned older man put his hand on his friend's shoulder and whispered back, "We have an old saying in the Duffy clan: If the br-r-rain had all the answers, there would be no need for God. Go with yer instincts, man. Follow yer heart. It and God will always lead you to the r-r-right place."

Appreciative of the advice, John David Sterling shook his friend's hand and, with his arm interlocked with the beautiful young lady of Haddington Moor, escorted her back up the long flight of concrete and tiled stairs to the dining facilities at King's Cross.

In spite of the open-air roof breached by a German bomb weeks earlier, life went on as usual at the quaint tearoom garden at the station. People emerged slowly from their bunkers and basements and returned to the streets and shops, and one of the premier restaurants of London. The young couple found a quiet corner. Mary Catherine sat opposite John David, who cautiously laid his briefcase with papers and secret contents against an adjoining wall. She ordered tea, he ordered coffee, and they chatted for hours about the weather, the current hit parade songs, and the latest news from America. It was Mary Catherine who broke the superficial small talk.

"I knew you weren't like the other Yanks the instant I heard your voice."

"Oh, and how is that?"

"Well, for one thing, you didn't use trite American colloquialisms like 'swell' and 'youse guys.' I knew there was something special about you. So, tell me, how did a Texas cowboy end up here in jolly old England?"

"Well, Miss, I guess a lot of it was Daddy's doing. He always had a tough time making ends meet as a rancher. The cattle business in West Texas is not for the faint of heart, let me assure you. He always wanted a better life for me than what he had gone through, so when I graduated from high school he drove me to Austin and pushed me out the door. Gave me a thousand dollars saved up and said, 'Son, I'll see you again in four years. Now, go make something of yourself. *Persevere.*' He pointed to the university and drove off. I knew right then and there that whatever I got out of life was up to me, and the Good Lord, so I got a part-time job and enrolled in the School of Engineering. I graduated in '42 but the Army Air Corp got ahold of me and, well, here I am."

"So, Captain, does this mean when the war is over you're going to be an engineer?"

"No, Ma'am. Daddy doesn't know it yet, but I'm going back to Rancho Rio Concho to help him raise cattle. You see, the ranch has been in the family for years. Great-granddaddy started it. Built everything with his own two hands. Shoot, even the kin are buried there. I'll be laid to rest there, too, I suppose. No way could I live with myself if I didn't carry on the family tradition—never really wanted to be an engineer, anyway. Always loved the cattle business. Guess I'm going to follow my heart and do what I think is right."

"Why, I think that's an admirable quality. I, too, feel there is nothing finer for a human soul than farming. My family for ten generations has been raising Black Angus. I love working all the farm chores: feeding the calves, herding-up the heifers, inoculating the bulls. It's more like play I'd say, than work. And, believe it or not, I especially love the smell of the barnyard as it mixes with freshly cut grass. I think farming appeals to all my senses—common sense especially." She smiled demurely, feeling at ease with her dashing captain. "We two appear to have some things in common. So let me ask you, Captain, how many acres does this ranch of yours have?"

Her question perturbed him but he also realized she didn't know the rules of cowboy etiquette.

"Miss," he paused, now feeling a tad too formal. "Would it be alright if I call you Miss Mary?"

"Why, that'll be just dandy, Captain. I like the ring of that."

"Well then, Miss Mary, let me interject. There are two things you should never ask a man from Texas. One is how many head of cattle he has. The other is how big his ranch is. In either case, you'll never get a straight answer and, besides, it's just plain bad manners. Sort of like asking a man how big a certain part of his anatomy is." As he continued to speak, he removed his aviator's cap and placed it on the table. A thick tuft of coal black hair fell across his eyes. The sight proved bothersome to Mary Catherine—the dangling locks distracting her from concentrating on his words and Texas drawl. In response, she licked her thumb and index finger and creased the strands of hair back in line with the others. At first, he flinched, unsure of the gesture. Yet, he also sensed her tenderness and gathered her free hand with his until she finished her coiffure attempts.

"I don't think that'll work," he muttered. "It's a cowlick."

"Nonsense," she replied. "Anything can be tamed, Captain Sterling."

"Please. Please call me *Cappy*. That's what all my friends call me. Never did care for John David or JD."

"Cappy, huh? I like that. I like that a lot."

"And just how many acres are there at your Haddington Moor?"

"Now, wait a minute, Cappy. Aren't you violating your own cowboy rules of civility?"

"Yes, Ma'am, but I threw all the rules out the moment I first laid eyes on you."

"Well, you bad boy, in that case I shall answer you. The MacLaren clan has a full square. And the grandest square in all the Lothians, I might add." She stated proudly.

"Just six hundred forty acres?" he winced.

"Not exactly. The Scottish people never accepted the old English customs and measurements. Our squares are slightly larger. We have a full eight hundred English acres in total." She beamed proudly. "We can support over twelve hundred head. Now, tell me, how big is yours?"

"How big is mine?"

"You know—how big your *ranch* is, dear Cappy. How many acres?"

"We have 30,000. Well, actually 30,640, if you count Uncle Frank's piece."

"Thirty thousand acres? My goodness. And what about this Uncle Frank?"

"That's Mama's brother. When Daddy and Mama got

married, he promised her that Uncle Frank could live on their land. Daddy kept his word but gave Uncle Frank the square out in the far northwest corner—fifteen miles away."

She laughed, clapping her hands together. "How positively delightful," she remarked. "This country of yours is so vast."

"So let me see if I understand your situation," he continued. "Your mother shipped you off to get an education and get you away from Scotland?"

"Not Scotland—our farm. Haddington Moor. You see, Cappy, I love the old place. I love farming and cattle raising, but my mother doesn't appreciate the same strong female pioneer spirit that has been captured in your Texas. And, I think what finally got to her was when she saw me helping my brother, James, castrate the bulls."

"You mean you actually cut their testicles off?"

"Snip, snip." She smiled, her two fingers mimicking a pair of scissors.

"Ouch." He grimaced in sympathy. "And she shipped you off to London just like that?" he asked, snapping his fingers.

"That's right. Just like that." She snapped her fingers in response. "It's been three years now and I've almost lost my brogue—*almost*."

"Well, that's downright horrible, Miss Mary. I can't imagine losing my Texas drawl even if I was shipped off to New York City."

"Nor I, Cappy. Nor I." She cooed, sighing at the sound of his accent.

"And you haven't been back to your place in three years, huh?"

"That's right. Mother said she'd bring me home and marry me off when I turn twenty. That's in a mere two months."

"She'd marry you to someone you don't even know?"

"Oh, heavens no, Cappy. She can say what she wants but

I am a woman of independent spirit. We Scottish lassies have been voting for years now, or haven't you heard?"

"Ah, yes—you're teasing me now, aren't you?"

"Just a little, Cappy."

Mary Catherine slipped one shoe off and began rubbing his calf under the table, hoping to perk his interest even more. He smiled sheepishly, a little wary of her advances and not sure if he liked losing control of his feelings. He had never felt this way before but war had a way of rushing the emotions. War had a way of forging strangers into lovers.

"But don't you miss Haddington Moor?" he pressed. "I miss Rancho Rio Concho something awful. I hate to admit it but for the past few months, late at night, I've even shed tears over the old place."

"Aye. And me, too. There's not a day that goes by, Cappy, when I don't dream of home and my secret place."

"Secret place?"

"A spot on the hill overlooking Haddington Moor, high above the farm house and barns that dot our parcel of green. It's a place I claimed as my very own. When I get homesick here in London, I close my eyes and repeat to myself three times the words, 'Haddington Moor,' and I'm silently transported in my mind's eye to the dearest and most wonderful piece of land in the world. There I sit and watch the endless heather meadows, the green of the moors, and the tiny thistle and white flowers of the early morning hours. I survey the rock hedges laid by my ancestors centuries ago. The endless pattern of stone fences crisscrosses the moors as if defying the landscape itself. And I smell the sweet aroma of the grasses and blossoms mixed with the barnyard odors. Best of all, I inhale the wonderful fragrance of the pink twinflowers. I love all those smells as they tease my senses into submission. And, as I'm lying on my hill the breeze picks up and pats my face and blows my hair over my shoulders. I can see the valley below me glistening from the

spring runoff and the dew sparkling like diamonds in the cut.
I can see the monarchs of the glen scampering in the distance
with fawns in pursuit of their mothers. All is well at
Haddington Moor. . . and that's what I do when I'm
homesick, Cappy. I simply close my eyes and dream of it.
Someday I'll take you to my secret place. I promise."

He reached across the table and handed her his
handkerchief.

"I hope yer not givin' me a used hankie. I hate crusty
buggers when I'm dryin' me tears," she sobbed, losing for a
moment her newly acquired proper English diction. "Now
I'm sounding like a farm girl, aren't I Cappy? I'm so sorry."

"No. That's all right. And the handkerchief—it's fresh. I
promise." He paused to let her regain her composure. "Miss
Mary, you must really love that farm of yours?"

"With all my heart and soul," she answered, blowing her
nose into the clean linen. "So, Cappy, tell me about your
land in the highlands of West Texas."

He drew a deep breath and glanced away for a moment.
Talking about Rancho Rio Concho was difficult. It forced
him to explore hidden sentiments shrouded by his manly
nature—feelings he had been taught to suppress. Yet, he also
sensed he could share any secret with her. He trusted her.
Looking deep into her eyes and with his hand clasping hers,
he began to describe the place he called home.

"We certainly don't have the green of Scotland you
described, Miss Mary. Shoot, anything green is probably
what grew under the manure. At Rancho Rio Concho, all we
have is the elements. Nature at her very best and very worst.
Everyday. If it's not the harsh cold of blue northers, it's the
hot summers baking a man's brains under his hat. The rain?
Shoot, the only time it rains is when you *don't* need it. It's a
totally unpredictable place. We even have a saying: If you
don't like today's weather, just wait until tomorrow. The one
constant you can count on is the vastness of the never-ending

blue sky that stretches beyond the horizon. It's a blue I've
never seen anywhere else. So clear, so pure. It's as if God
papered heaven with the ocean and tacked it right above
Texas. It's magnificent, especially when the sun goes down.
You've never seen the colors of the rainbow splashed on the
horizon like in our sunsets. It's because of the dust. I call it
West Texas *magic* dust. It gets hung in the clouds and in the
evening skies, and changes the color of everything as
daylight fades. The sun's rays riot in violence with each
sunset. And talk about flowers. From March to May, Texas
erupts in the most brilliant display of wildflowers known to
humanity. It's like the scene in the *Wizard of Oz* when
they're running through the poppy field. You'd love those
wildflowers. I just know it." He took another sip of coffee.
"But, the land itself? It's not good for much. That's probably
why you have to own so darn much of it to get a decent
yield. But, when it does yield, it makes you thank God for
what belongs to you—you and the cattle, that is. Once a year
we gather the herds in a roundup and that's when you really
begin to appreciate the land. As we herd the steers let out to
roam the range for months at a stretch, to reproduce and
fatten, as we start to bring them in, their numbers just keep
growing and growing and growing. By the time we're
driving 'em into the stock pens, their numbers have swollen
to over 7,000, and it's like a miracle because just ten months
earlier we only released 5,000. Let me tell you, there's no
prettier sight than the longhorns coming home after a drive.
They're the toughest and grandest beasts known to a
cowboy. . . ."

She watched his eyes sparkle as he told her more about
his special place north of a town called San Angelo. She had
never met anyone who shared a passion for land as strongly
as her own.

They were still holding hands at midnight when the waiter

told them the tearoom had closed and they must leave. Their food was cold and had not been touched.

"Where do we go now, Miss Mary?"

"My flat," she responded. "My roommate is out of town. We'll have the entire place to ourselves and we can chat all night."

He grabbed the briefcase, carefully protecting its contents.

"Secret war papers, Cappy?"

"No. Tequila—you know, Mexican hooch."

"H-m-m-m, I've heard of it from the movies but I've never seen any of it here in Great Britain."

"You're right. Nobody here has any. Daddy sends me a bottle once a month. Unfortunately, it doesn't last very long."

When they reached her fifth floor apartment, through gasps of breath he commented he could sure use a "stiff drink."

"That's a splendid idea. I've always wanted to try tequila. What do you drink it in?"

"Nothing special. Just straight up in short glasses or what we call shot glasses."

"Ah, yes. We call them drams," she said while searching her kitchen cabinets for the correct type of vessel. "Oh, poop, Cappy. All I have fitting the description is Mother's small demitasse cups."

"That'll do just fine," he reassured. "For her sake, why don't we pretend it's *hardy English coffee*? We wouldn't want to upset her, would we?"

"Aye, Cappy. 'Hardy English coffee' it is. Now all we need to do is toast the occasion. It's a Scottish tradition of celebration. Brings good luck to all who partake."

He laid his unfilled cup back down. A sickened look overpowered his face.

"Are you all right, Cappy?"

"I'm fine. It's just—it's just the last time I drank to someone's health, it was to one of my best friends. He was heading off on a mission. His twenty-fifth. He was scheduled to return stateside when his plane was blown out of the sky. I was told they never found his body." He paused to gather his composure. "Not sure if I ever want to toast any occasion again after that experience."

Then, Captain John David Sterling became melancholy. He'd had his fill of war and death. War ran counter to his gentle free-spirited nature. He knew with each additional mission, he increased the chances of never returning home to his ranch. Toasts of good fortune, he thought, had nothing to do with improving his chances of survival.

"Sometimes when I'm flying a mission, I look at my crew and in some strange way it reminds me of the cattle drives back on the ranch. There I am, riding tall in the saddle of a powerful B-17, pushing the crew onward just like they were cattle themselves. Even lowly steers know they're going to die and that I'm driving them to the slaughterhouse, yet, they still trust me to bring them in safely to the certainty of death. When you're flying so close to heaven, the odds are stacked against you. I sense my crew realize I'm driving them to the slaughter—they trust me just like the cattle. Ironic isn't it?"

At first, Mary Catherine didn't know how to respond to his melancholy. Without thinking, she threw herself into his arms in a tight embrace. Her cheek pressed against his in an attempt to console his distraught feelings. "Cappy, dearest Cappy. You are not leading your crew to the certainty of their death. Every time you bring them home, you're defying the odds—you're defying life, itself. When that happens it should be a time for celebration and praise. So, I don't want to hear any more gloomy talk from the likes of you."

"And just why not?" he whispered, looking deep into her eyes.

"Because—because you have your land and me to come

back to, John David Sterling. Now, I want you to come up with a toast just for us so every time you return from a mission we can celebrate the accomplishment with praise."

"All right, Miss Mary. A toast it is but it won't be about the land or to the future."

"So, what will it be about?"

"It'll be about you."

"Oh, nonsense, Cappy. There are things far more worthy of acclamation than myself."

"Right now, I can't think of any, but if you like, I'll throw in a little Robert Burns to keep the tradition properly Scottish."

"You've heard of Robert Burns?"

"Aye, me bonnie lassie. In my high school drama class I had to memorize and recite his poems. So, pour us the 'hardy English coffee,' Miss Mary, and let me toast you tonight and if I make it back from my next mission, I'll toast you again."

"And again and again," she added gleefully, "until there's no more war."

"Until the cows come home."

"Until the cows come home it is," she exclaimed.

He remembered his verses and he toasted her for the very first time on that late night in far away London, alone in her flat. Their demitasse cups gently clanged together and they swallowed hard on their *coffee*. He leaned over and kissed her full on the lips. She responded and their lives were never the same again.

Weeks later, by his twenty-fifth mission, their love affair had become so intense Mary Catherine insisted on maintaining sentry by the airfield fence to await his bomber's return. Counting the planes as they landed, straining for a glimpse of his insignia, she realized she could never live without her Cappy. After each mission, he toasted her. After each toast, they made love.

The success of the very last mission, however, was not a cause for celebration. Unless he re-upped, he would be sent home. She feared the worst if he continued flying, so when his orders came through sending him back to America, he gracefully bowed out of the war and prepared to bid Great Britain goodbye. It was at their small pub in Mayfair where he proposed marriage.

"Come back to Texas and live with me," he begged.

"I love you so very much, Cappy. I can't think of anything except you. It's just that my heart is with Haddington Moor, in the Lothians. Certainly, you should understand those feelings. Land has a way of holding onto your heart and never letting go. How could I be happy elsewhere?"

"Because you'll be with me, Miss Mary, and I'll give you babies in Texas that will occupy your thoughts and your time. When I come home at night, we'll make love. When I get up in the morning, before I steal to the fields, we'll make love. Between the children and the lovemaking, you'll never have time to think of Haddington Moor. So, marry me, my bonnie lassie."

"I simply can't live without you, dearest Cappy, but Haddington Moor won't be easy to get over. You must promise me two things if I should leave Scotland."

"Anything. Just name them."

"First, I want you to promise that someday you'll bring me back to Haddington Moor. I could never leave this world without seeing my birthright again. I could never be at peace without looking out upon the green from my secret lookout."

"I promise," he stated unflinchingly.

"And second, I want you to swear you'll never forget the tradition you and I have begun here, the Scottish ways of celebrating life through a toast and through praise. Our children and their children must grow up knowing these ways. We must take a bit of Scotland to the new world with us so it lives forever in the hearts of our kin."

"Miss Mary, I promise you that our wonderful tradition will live forever. And, I can also assure you that nothing will ever stop me from bringing you back to Scotland. After all, I am a man of my word."

My heart's in the Highlands, my heart is not here,
My heart's in the Highlands a chasing the deer;
Chasing the wild deer and following the roe,
My heart's in the Highlands, wherever I go.

Robert Burns

FOUR

(1996)

It was close to midnight, five hours after the cowboys galloped over Little Concho Ridge. The day's excitement and rigorous dinner preparation had taken their toll on Mary Catherine. As she watched Cappy drying the dishes, not sure how best to break the news about the illness, she knew the truth could no longer be hidden. She had already lost ten pounds and was showing signs of gauntness; the coughing and relentless hacking refused to let up. He would realize her condition soon enough. Best to tell him now, she thought, rather than some young intern at the county hospital or a paramedic attempting to resuscitate. Nevertheless, the first words belonged to him on this late night vigil with the dishes.

"Miss Mary, I read James' letter you left on the kitchen table. I feel bad about his and Angus' situation. I feel so useless. Maybe we can get a loan from our bank and—"

"Cappy, don't be silly. We've just turned a good year here. There's no more room for debt. If Haddington Moor is to survive, it simply will. If not, then it wasn't meant to be."

"But there's got to be something—"

"*No*. No, Cappy. There's nothing we can do."

He studied her face. It was tired and exhausted. The years in Texas had robbed the youth from his beautiful Scottish rose. Her eyes had lost their glow. He knew hidden beneath the tough veneer, deep down inside, she was grieving over her land so far away. Why wouldn't she let him help her brother? he wondered. They had always managed to survive financial hardships at the ranch. They could survive this one, too. Had she lost her fight? Had she lost her will to defy the odds?

"Something is wrong. I sense it, Mary Catherine. We've been together far too long on our journey for you not to share whatever it is that's on your mind. You can tell me anything. Anything at all."

"Yes, I know," she whispered without looking into his eyes.

"Then, do tell me, sweet Mary. I've got the strength of a thousand lifetimes. Enough to handle anything good or bad that's on your mind. Talk to me, sweet wife."

She wiped her hands on her apron and untied it from behind her back. Taking a deep breath, she moved to him, holding his hand in the same manner they had so innocently held hands that very first night together.

"Cappy, I don't quite know where to begin." She paused, wiping away tears. "I'm sick, dearest husband, very sick and I don't have much time."

He said nothing but settled into a kitchen chair. He had suspected for some time she had been ill but the shock of knowing the truth wounded him to the marrow. And then, without warning, he began to cry. He pressed his head against the flat of her stomach. She ran her fingers through his hair and patted him on the shoulder.

"Don't cry, dearest Cappy. Please don't cry. We've tamed life, you and me, for lo these many years. We can tame heaven, too."

As she spoke, a tuft of his sparse gray hair fell across his forehead and over his eyes. She licked her thumb and index finger with her saliva and brushed it back in line with the others. Soon the hair re-collapsed. He said nothing.

"Anything can be tamed," she whispered. "Anything can be tamed."

As the days passed, a steady procession of family and friends made their way back to the ranch to pay respects to the grand dame of Rancho Rio Concho.

"I don't understand what all this fuss is about. I'm not dead yet, for heaven's sake. And besides, I've lived a long rich life, full of the best of everything," Mary Catherine said, trying to convince Cappy and family members how life without her presence would still go on. Still, she had become progressively weaker and had trouble standing for long uninterrupted periods. Time was running out and Cappy had to make a decision.

Earlier, he had called a hastily put together meeting of the family. Now, while they were inside the house waiting on him, he had to make one final amend with the *other* family members and find peace in the decision he made. So, he stole to the family burial plot to touch his father's headstone, confessing his feelings to the ghosts of the past.

"Daddy, I know how much this place meant to you. When times got tough, I thought about selling it. More than once. The thing is, you always told me to never give up. To *persevere*. 'Always persevere, John David,' is what you said and I did just that. With Steven's help, I turned the ranch around. Making good money now, too, I might add. Seems kinda poetic, doesn't it? Finally doing well. Then, I sell it. I just hope you and Mama, and the rest understand. I really love this place with all my heart but I love Miss Mary, too and I'm doing it for her because I gave her my word years ago. And you're the one who taught me that a man's word is everything—"

Cappy barely noticed Emilio walk up from behind and tap him on the shoulder. "You all right, Cappy? Come on, everyone's waiting. After all, you're the one who called this family meeting."

"I'll be right there, son. I just need another minute."

Emilio's face wrinkled. "Look, Cappy, if it's about Miss Mary—"

"No, it's about something else. I'll be there shortly."

Emilio left, having a queasy feeling about what the old cowboy was about to announce. Cappy abuptly turned to look at his great-grandfather's grave marker.

"Thank you, sir, for the opportunity. I sure am awfully sorry about all this."

When Cappy entered the dining room, the three cowboys were assembled around Mary Catherine. She was the first to speak up.

"Cappy, couldn't this meeting have waited until the boys finished their chores?"

"Afraid not, Miss Mary. This is pretty important. I've got some news. Something I need to share with you all. You see, I've sold the ranch. Sold her outright for cash to Zack. He always wanted this place and he gave me a darned good price."

The boys were speechless. They thought the ranch would always be there for them, even after Mary Catherine was gone. Even after their grandfather had passed away.

"But why, Grandpa? Why? I thought you wanted us to carry on the family tradition here?" Steven asked.

"I do, but I'm also a man of my word. You see, when I married your grandma I made her two promises. The second was to bring her back to Haddington Moor someday. This may be my only chance."

"But, Cappy, you can't give up this place. You love this place as much as life itself," Mary Catherine pleaded.

"Miss Mary, I love you more than life itself. This place has sustained our family for years and served its purpose. Now it's time to move on."

"Now wait a minute, Grandpa. I went to college and worked my tail off so I could run it. Before I came here, you were losing money left and right. Now we're making money. Are you telling me that all my hard work has been a waste of time? That now I don't get my chance? What am I suppose to do?" Steven pressed.

"No, it wasn't a waste. You'll get your chance, Steven. Maybe it won't be here in Texas but you'll get it. I promise. Just have a little faith."

"*Faith*? Hell, I put all my faith in you and you just stabbed me in the back. How could you?"

"Shut-up, Steven. Let Grandpa finish," Nate cut in.

By now, Cappy's emotions were running high. He was angered by Steven's outburst but knew his grandson's sentiment was correct. He never bothered to consult his partner on the decision. The whole thing got dropped on the lad without any forethought.

"Look, boys. Haddington Moor is as much a part of this family's past as this ranch. In fact, it's been in your blood a lot longer. Ten generations. If we don't help her out, she won't be around for your children and that would be a real tragedy. As of today, we've barely got one month to rescue her or the bank takes over. This time James and Angus need more than our money. They need our livestock and the very best this family has to offer—*our know-how*. That means all three of you are needed, that is, if you're up to the challenge."

Emilio asked, "But what's going to happen to the horses and to Pedo?"

On hearing his name, the cow dog yelped and leaped on

the table where he could become the center of attention.

"They're all going to be needed. We'll ship them along with our best cattle."

The three cowboys looked at each other. No one knew quite what to say but it was evident Cappy was not about to change his mind. Mary Catherine grabbed her husband's hand and sobbed. "It's all my fault. It's all my fault."

"Shoot, Miss Mary. Things happen for a reason. Maybe it was just our destiny to come to Haddington Moor's aid."

"Can we bring Sir Charles, too?" she asked, breaking a smile between her tears.

"That old bird? You want to bring that roadrunner to Scotland? I don't think he can survive there."

"Cappy, if Sir Charles can survive West Texas, he can survive anywhere, including the moors of Scotland."

"Whatever you say, Miss Mary. Whatever you want."

"And I want us to bring his girlfriend, too."

"I suppose you've named her as well?"

"Aye. Her name's Camilla."

Everyone around the table broke out in guarded laughter, except Steven. It was Little Nate, however, who decided to be the first cowboy to show support.

"All right, everyone listen up. Nobody wants to leave the ranch but maybe Grandpa's right. Now the way I look at it, the odds are stacked against us, but if we all work together," he paused, eyeing Steven, "we can make this thing work. I just know we can. And, I've never known the Sterlings to back away from a challenge. So gather up. Squeeze in here and stack your hands on top of mine. Starting today we've got a new tradition."

The four men and Mary Catherine obeyed him, interlacing their hands one upon the other. Steven was the last to join in.

"We may be Sterlings by name but we're also MacLarens," Nate continued. "The blood of both families runs through our veins. So tell me. Who does Haddington Moor belong to? *The bank?*"

There was a brief silence. No one knew quite what to say. Finally, Mary Catherine spoke up. "No. It belongs to us, Nathaniel—the Sterlings and the MacLarens. That's our land."

Nate smiled, nodding his head. His grandmother understood what he wanted.

"I can't hear you-u-u," he sang, admonishing the family members who remained silent. He challenged everyone a second time. "Who does Haddington Moor belong to?"

"That's our land," they said together, first looking at Nate and then, at one another.

"Louder," he yelled.

"That's our land," they said, raising their voices in unison. Even Pedo joined in, howling with the humans.

"Louder."

"THAT'S OUR LAND."

"Louder. . . ."

Far out on the highway running south to San Angelo, a noise could be heard above the wind driven rustle of scrub and cactus, and above the chirping of the cardinals—a joyful noise of men and beasts defying the odds. Anyone who dared to take Haddington Moor would have to fight the family first.

Five thousand miles away, a wry middle-aged man resplendent in a well-tailored Armani suit stood by his car at the gated rock entrance to a small cattle farm. He had been surveying the landscape through binoculars for some time and appeared out of patience. His idling Bentley's exhaust fumes snaked past the rock hedge separating the road from the surrounding lush fields, and fanned out into the pasture for hundreds of yards. Now finished with his survey, he tucked the binoculars under an arm and unzipped a black leather notebook. A scrolled paper immediately unraveled to the ground. The heading on the printout read: Lowlands Oil—White Castle Project. The list contained the names of cattle farms in receivership by alphabetical order; a second column contained the words 'cattle count.' The man deftly screwed open a Mont Blanc pen with one hand while pointing down the list of names until he found what he was looking for.

"Ah, there you are—Haddington Moor Cattle Farm."

In the second column he wrote the word 'NONE.' Just as quickly, he re-scrolled the paper, re-zipped the notebook, and climbed into the Bentley. Once inside the acoustic comforts of his elegant vehicle, he slid the *Queen* CD in the stereo player and cranked up the volume so he couldn't hear the gravel spraying the gated entrance as the Bentley accelerated away.

"*Another-one-bites-the-dust*," he sang enthusiastically, forgetting for the moment the havoc his employer created.

Reunion

With Mary, when shall we return,
Seek pleasure to renew;
Quoth Mary, Love, I like the burn,
And I shall follow you.

Robert Burns

FIVE

Either the vibration of the steel bulwark woke Cappy or the back and forth pitching of anti-acid tablets on the credenza separating their beds. Whichever the cause, it made little difference at 3:00AM. Fully stirred, Cappy could not get back to sleep and decided it best to arise. Fumbling through the darkness, he groped for his freshly creased jeans. No light dared be turned on for fear of disturbing the slumber Mary Catherine desperately needed.

The voyage on the cargo liner was nearing a conclusion as the ship had already steamed around the eastern coast of England and now steered north for Edinburgh. The sixteen days at sea were difficult for Mary Catherine but she and the boys refused to leave Cappy's side. He insisted on escorting the cattle and Ben. For him it seemed the right thing to do. Severing the bond between man and beast had never been an easy thing for him. They, too, were family, he said. So, in the early morning hours, like the fifteen nights before, Cappy rose to steal to the cargo hold deep within the ship's belly to inspect the cattle and share a private moment with his longhorn. Before leaving, he felt Mary Catherine's forehead.

She was cool to the touch; the remnants of fever had been
broken with antibiotics supplied by the ship's doctor.
Relieved, he tiptoed out of the room with boots in-hand but,
when he unlatched the door, the hallway light flooded the
still of the cabin. He glanced back inside to make sure Mary
Catherine's sleep remained undisturbed. Fortunately, the
only pair of eyes watching his departure belonged to Pedo.
He hand signaled a come-hither sign, the one Mary
Catherine had taught him, and the blue heeler leaped to his
side, fanning the thick salt air with an unruly tail. Then, he
slowly latched the door and sealed the cold metal with a
patted warm touch.

"I didn't think you'd want me to leave you behind," he
whispered while stroking Pedo's perked ears.

Truth be known, Cappy had long given up the inner
debate whether or not it was sane to talk to his friends, the
animals. When he turned sixty he capitulated, announcing he
could do "whatever he felt like," and, thus, decided it was
time to emerge from the 'closet' as one of those human
species openly practicing verbal communication with four-
legged creatures. It became a closely guarded family secret.
Now, eighteen years later, the only debate was whether he
heard the animals talk back—a debate with no resolution.

After stumbling to the stairway, Cappy pulled on his
boots. Pedo had memorized his master's routine and, on-
queue, sat up begging.

"Oh, all right. Hold your horses."

Cappy tossed his dog friend a ginger snap. Pedo caught
the treat without leaving the ground, and swallowed it whole,
yelping for more.

"Hush up, Pedo. We don't want to wake anyone,
especially Miss Mary."

To keep the dog pacified, Cappy tossed a second and
third treat. Satisfied Pedo would remain quiet with food in
his mouth, they began the long descent down a seemingly

endless flight of stairs. With each landing, the disjoint cadence of the engines rattled Cappy's senses more viciously; the vibrations of the propellers unnerved Pedo, spooking the dog into a bug-eyed panic. When they finally reached the watertight hatch inscribed 'AUTHORIZED PERSONNEL ONLY,' the descent came to an end.

"Whew. I'm glad we won't have to tackle those stairs after today. Hey, Pedo?"

This time Pedo decided to remain silent on the subject and not yelp. It made little difference. Cappy was sure his friend's frightened eyes said something to the effect of, "Damn straight, boss man." The dog's reluctance to utter real words had always been fine by Cappy. Pedo's expressive eyes said as much as any man ever needed to hear.

Inside, the dark hold packed tight with cattle. All five hundred remained healthy after the long journey. At first the smell of manure and urine overwhelmed Cappy, so he kept the door ajar to re-circulate air. Once the stairwell air seeped in, he fumbled for the light switch and threw down the handle. The room instantly ignited white by three powerful 1500-watt bulbs. The cattle recoiled from the shock of the brilliance and bawled in pain.

"Good morning," Cappy called out.

Again, there was no intelligible reply. Some muted bawling by Brangus bulls kept too close to heifers echoed from the back of the hold. All else remained silent.

"You boys will get plenty of that in due course," Cappy mumbled, referring to the bulls' needs. "Just hang in there a little longer. We'll be there soon enough."

As he worked his way down the narrow pen separating the two genders, he eventually wound his way to the solitary pen with the thick straw bed and the overhead fan. The suite belonged to Ben the bull.

"Good morning to you, Ben. How you doing today, old boy?"

Ben had been lying down for days. The slow roll of the ship upset his equilibrium and he felt more at ease on his belly than on all fours.

"Look what I brought you, Ben," Cappy said, holding out a ginger snap.

The longhorn pressed its drippy nose through the slats of the pen and sniffed the cookie. He licked it to assure himself nothing had changed from the night before or the night before that. While trustworthy, the animal never acted completely at ease around humans. Soon enough, the hesitancy buckled and he snatched the ginger snap, grinding it with cud and consuming in less than ten seconds. An exhilarating snort moistened the rancher's hand. Cappy wiped the excretions on his jeans and patted his friend on the head. "I know this trip's been hard on you, Ben. I'm awfully sorry. And I know how much you're going to miss Texas. Shoot, we're all going to miss Texas, but you and me, we're doing the right thing by Miss Mary, and I'm counting on you to help me pull off a miracle when we get to Scotland."

Cappy turned to face the other cattle that by now had become attentive.

"You all listen up and listen up good. I've been saving this speech for the last day on this ship and today's the day— I'm sure most of you didn't know this but your actual origins are from Scotland. You Texas Brangus, half your bloodline comes through your cousins the Aberdeen-Angus cattle, and from over one hundred twenty-five years ago. You Galloway heifers don't even need a kilt since you're as Scottish as one can get, or so that's what Steven tells me. Even you, Ben, have roots from the moors. Anyway, we're all connected somehow or another to this new home of ours. The place is in our blood and in our hearts—or at least it should be. And we've all got something at stake by making this thing work. Now, I'm counting on all of you to do good by your ancestors because they're dying off from disease. You're not only the hope of Haddington Moor, you're the future of the Scottish cattle business. And between shipping you and everything else overseas and bailing out Haddington Moor, we're stone-broke. So, there's nowhere else for us to go. Now, any of you got questions?" he asked, wincing at the question itself. Cappy knew logically that no one sane would hear anything. Glancing around the hold at their silent faces, he sensed his sanity remained intact.

As he turned out the lights, a strange hush fell over his five hundred children. Maybe they did understand, he thought. Maybe they really understood this journey was for Miss Mary. Then, he climbed the long flight of stairs with Pedo and stole back to bed before Mary Catherine would wake.

By 6:00AM, the sun had risen on what would be the first of many cloudless mornings. The ship pulled within two miles of the coastline to round the upper cape into the Firth of Forth, the narrow strait leading into Edinburgh harbor and their ultimate destination, the piers of Leith. The ensemble of Texans gathered on the deck to view the shoreline and marvel at the green of their new homeland. Mary Catherine, confined to a wheelchair, wrapped in a Shetland blanket. The others dressed in the only garb they understood: boots, jeans, heavily starched dress shirts, and cowboy hats, which they held to counter the stiff gale. As they watched the sights, the ship skirted two enormous rock outcrops protruding from the calm morning waters. Little Nate broke the silence.

"Grandma, look at those things. They look like volcanoes or something."

"Aye. That they are. They're inactive now. Have been for some time. In Gaelic they were described as 'the ancient ones,' but now they're simply known as the *laws*," she said, clutching her blanket to keep it from flapping in the breeze.

Cappy spotted a lone monolith off in the distance. "Now

there's a beautiful law," he remarked, pointing to a steep vertical hill towering behind a coastal town.

"That's Berwick Law. The one in your poem to me—your toast."

"Well, I'll be. I had no idea what Berwick Law was. Never thought I'd see the darned thing. That's for sure."

"Well, dearest, on a clear morning if you look to the northeast from Haddington Moor, you can also see it in the distance. As a wee girl, I used to spy it from my secret lookout. I always knew when I could see Berwick Law, the weather would be good and the day would be long."

He took her hand in his, understanding now what Robert Burns had meant in the poetry written so many years before. It was a wonderful revelation, he thought.

"Cappy, have you decided how we're going to sneak Sir Charles and Camilla through Customs?" she asked.

"Not really, Miss Mary. I guess I've been too preoccupied with the cattle. I do believe we're going to have a real problem getting those birds approved."

"Don't worry, dear husband. I've already come up with a solution. Come closer so I can tell you."

As he bent down, she cupped a hand close to his ear and whispered the plan. After she divulged the ruse, he stood and shook his head in disbelief.

"You always keep me on my toes, Miss Mary."

"Tell me the secret, too, Grandma," Little Nate pleaded.

"No, Nathaniel. It's best you're not an accomplice to the high treasonous crime of bird smuggling."

Minutes later, and with Nate obnoxiously begging on his hands and knees, Mary Catherine still refused to reveal the secret. Steven tried ignoring the commotion his cousin stirred. He turned around to face the wind headlong and fired off a question to Cappy. "Have you seen Emilio this morning?" he asked Cappy, diverting everyone's attention.

"Last I saw him, he was about to use the ship-to-shore

radio to call Lupe."

"That so? Doesn't surprise me. I think Emilio misses Lupe too much to stay put in Scotland. We'll be hurting if he returns home."

"And if he doesn't stay, that's fine," Mary Catherine interjected. "Love can do that to you, Steven. It can call you from thousands of miles and make you do things counter to your very character," she added, squeezing Cappy's hand.

"Yup, ain't that the truth," Nate teased. "Why, I've heard it can even drive you crazy. Make you start talking to cattle."

"Now, we're not going to get into that so early in the morning are we?" Cappy remarked, perturbed anyone knew about his nightly vigils with the animals.

"Well, Grandpa, we all know you've been talking to Big Ben again. Grandma got a report from the captain. He says you've been sneaking down to the hold in the middle of the night and talking up a storm."

Embarrassed, Cappy looked away and out to the shoreline. "One of these days maybe you'll understand," he retorted. "You'll understand why I do it."

As he spoke, the ship pitched to port and made a final turn past the lighthouse at Fidra. They remained by the rail the entire way, watching the sights and sounds unfurl as they approached Edinburgh and the Pier of Leith.

By noon, Old Rover had been driven off the ship's ramp and cleared Custom's inspection. The cattle and horses, however, remained penned and quarantined for forty-eight hours before being available for shipment to Haddington Moor. Cappy supervised the herding of the *children* to their new land based stockades adjoining the dock. He gave Big Ben final instructions before rejoined the other family members waiting to pass the last checkpoint. The three boys walked behind him as he pushed Mary Catherine in her wheelchair through a metal detector. Pedo squirmed in her arms when the alarm went off, but Cappy continued pushing as though he heard nothing.

"Excuse me, Mum," the agent shouted, intercepting them ten feet past the detector. "I'm afr-r-raid I'm going to have to ask ya to walk through the detector and—"

"Inspector, as you can see my wife is gravely ill. She can't walk anymore," Cappy interjected. "You see, we've come all the way from Texas to bring her back home to Haddington Moor. Perhaps you've heard of it? It's about—"

Cappy had no sooner gushed his well-rehearsed lines when the two, caged roadrunners stashed underneath Mary Catherine's wheelchair and curtained by her skirt, burst out singing two rapid squeals, "R-r-r-r-r-r, R-r-r-r-r-r."

"Good heavens, man. What was that?" the customs agent startled before firing off the question, spinning away from Cappy and staring at Mary Catherine.

"It's. . . It's. . . ."

"It's her gas," Little Nate stated, whispering in the man's ear. "With her illness she passes wind all the time. You know, *passes gas.*"

The inspector glared at Nate with one eye. "Here, lad, we call it farting."

Nate leaned over. "She hates that word, sir."

"I understand. No problem, lad. You folks just have a nice day and I'm sorry to hear of your illness, Mum."

The Sterlings hastily loaded the Defender with their belongings, including the unruly chaparrals. Once in the Land Rover Mary Catherine turned to Little Nate. "You saved the day, Nathaniel. Whatever did you say to that man that he let us right through?"

"You really don't want to know, Grandma. Besides, it's a secret."

It was an elderly security guard at the gate exit who had the last laugh. "Good afternoon, folks. Care if I have a looksee?" he asked, eyeing Old Rover. "This is certainly a

fine machine," he crowed, feeling the weathered side doors
on the antique.

As Mary Catherine watched him fondle the car,
something about his mischievous blue eyes and craggy face
stirred a memory.

"It's a '53," she hollered out the back window while
trying to conceal the caged birds. "It once belonged to my
father. He was the thane of Haddington Moor."

"Ah-h-h-h, he must have been the head of the MacLaren
clan," the guard responded. "Robert MacAllister is the name.
Used to live not too far from there meself."

"*Robert MacAllister*? Why, I used to sit for a young rascal
of a lad years ago by the name of Little Robbie MacAllister,"
she hollered.

The guard looked into her eyes and smiled. "My goodness
gracious. You must be none other than Mary Catherine who
used to read bedtime stories to me."

"Aye, dear Robbie, aye. I knew it was you the minute I
spotted those blue eyes of yours."

"Well, I'm not the bad little boy I used to be, Mary
Catherine."

"Indeed, I should hope not."

"As a matter of fact, I've been so good that after next
week I'll be collecting me retirement pension. 'Been an
honest civil servant for lo the past forty-five years."

"Good for you, dear Robbie. I knew you always had it in
ya to do well in life."

She reached in her purse and took out a ginger snap.
Sliding the window open, she handed it to him and squeezed
his forearm.

"You're a good boy, Robbie MacAllister. Now, you be
sure and wash that down with one of those sugar-free
drinks."

"Yes, Mum," he answered. "Yes, Mum and—"

As the Sterlings sped out the gate, they never looked back

or heard Little Robbie finish his sentence, "—and those are a right bonnie, wee pair of roadrunners you've got there."

They drove south along the Firth of Forth waterway until the road widened into a divided six-lane highway that ushered them past landmarks Mary Catherine once memorized as a child.

"Any of this look familiar?" Steven asked as he drove.

"Some of it does but the city has changed so much that even the old haunts seem barely recognizable," she stated, feeling detached from the landscape. This was not how she remembered her Scotland. The fast food signs, the billboards, the malls, the bumper-to-bumper stretches of multicolored autos, and the endless rows of suburban townhouses were never a part of her memories. She felt as though time had erased the very best of her Lothian valley's history. "No, this certainly isn't the Edinburgh I remember. It feels as though it's changed to the likes of America." She sighed as they whizzed passed a McDonald's restaurant.

"They even have MTV here, Grandma. That ought to be good news for you and Pedo," added Nate.

"Oh, how wonderful," she said, her voice void of any real enthusiasm.

As she looked out the window, Emilio sensed her forlorn feelings and held her hand. "Miss Mary, I know you don't like what you're seeing here, that it's all changed, but I'm sure when we get to Haddington Moor it'll be exactly as you remember."

"Thank you, dear boy. I hope you're right. I hope you're right."

"Sure he's right," added Cappy. "Farms don't change. Just the people who inherit them. Now, I want you to wear your best face, Miss Mary, because Brother James, nephew Angus, and all your cousins will be there to greet us. I understand he's got a party planned in your honor—

something he called a *ceilidh*."

"A ceilidh is a festive social gathering of the clan. Knowing James, it'll be quite a party." She paused. "He certainly has been a good brother all these years, hasn't he, Cappy?"

"The best. The best there is. We just have to teach his boy, Angus, how to make money in the cattle business. Right, Steven?"

"That's right, Grandpa. We'll teach him."

"Aye, you're all good boys," she said, squeezing each on the shoulder. "I'm so very proud of you all."

Old Rover sped down the highway, accelerating like a seasoned steed returning to the barn. The further they escaped Edinburgh, the more familiar the sights became to Mary Catherine. By the time they exited off the expressway, where it intersected the town of Haddington, the men had been marveling at the profusion of healthy green pastures and abundance of water flowing in the Tyne River. The Concho River never flowed like that, they said, even in the best of times.

"Steven, turn left just beyond Lennoxlove House. Follow the signs to the town of Garvald," Mary Catherine instructed.

Once they neared Haddington Moor, she perked in anticipation. The twenty-nine mile journey from Edinburgh took a mere forty minutes with the aid of much improved roadbeds, nearly half the time it had taken when she last made the journey. The speed of the ride caught her unprepared. "Oh, goodness, Cappy, we're almost there. How do I look? Is my makeup in place? Do I need to brush my hair?"

"You're asking the wrong man, Grandma," Nate broke in. "You should be asking me my opinion because I've got better taste than Grandpa. Besides, who do you want to look good for—the old geezers or the young studs?"

"Well, the last time I was home, I tried to look good for

the young men but that was before I met your grandfather."

"In that case, here's the opinion of one handsome young man: you look hot. Real hot. I hope when I'm your age I look as—"

"Radiant," Steven interjected, scowling at his cousin.

"No, I'd say *hermosa*." Emilio winked.

"Utterly beautiful. Just like the very first time I laid eyes on you," Cappy stated.

"Yeah, that's right. All that stuff, too, Grandma. And *hot*," Nate continued, hoping to get the last word in.

When they got to Garvald, Mary Catherine had Steven turn south where the signs pointed to White Castle Fortress. The three-mile-long road deteriorated into a mélange of potholed blacktop patched after the passing of each winter.

"You never told me you lived next door to a castle, Grandma," Nate remarked.

"Aye. When I was growing up it was just part of my everyday life. I never gave a second thought to the rich history behind it. It was just there like the landscape. It blended in with everything else that seemed to have been around forever and a day."

When they passed over the brook known as Fen Burn, Old Rover screeched to a halt. The dirt and gravel drive leading away from the roadside was marked with a solitary sign 'Haddington Moor Cattle Farm.' Down the drive and off in the distance, barns and pens dotted the valley. The two-story rock and stucco farmhouse gleamed white against the green hills; its short front door bloated a cheerful bright red. A gray slate roof protruded out and over the house outer walls, providing a distanced runoff for the wet winter and spring rains. Not a single tree sprouted anywhere in the compound or grew in the valley, itself. The thick green meadow resembled an expanse of tundra or Nebraska rolling prairie. Where the valley spread south, it crested into two steep but separate hillsides nearly four hundred feet in height. Behind them lay a taller range of hills and behind them the towering Lammermuir Range that separated the Lothian region from the Borders. It was desolate land ruled by thick grass, heather, and stone hedges.

"Kind of looks like our ranch except no rocks and a lot of green grass," Nate quipped.

"No rocks?" Mary Catherine countered. "My heavens, Nathaniel, the rocks are there. Believe me. They are there. It's just after centuries of clearing the fields, the rocks aren't as plentiful as they once were. All those stones were laid one upon the other by the hands of the MacLarens, and stacked into the smart rows of hedge fence you see about you. Those rocks each have a history of their own. They kept in the cattle and kept out the English. The English and their government could never touch our cattle as long as—"

"Grandma, I think I see some people waving to us from the farmhouse," Steven interrupted. "Shouldn't we drive on in?"

"Yes. By all means. Just let me savor the view a little longer."

Emilio and Cappy were both right, she thought. The place had not changed a bit. The land was the same. Only the tenants had changed. Some were older. Some had new faces she had never seen. Others were still waiting their turn to toil the ground and make their mark. Soon, she would join the ones who had once attempted to tame the land but had passed on. Like her parents and their parents, she, too, would simply be referred to as an 'ancestor,' for there was nothing more sacred to the clan than ancestors. The emotion of the moment overpowered her and she wept openly, realizing the fifty-one year odyssey had finally ended. She was home.

"No use waiting here any longer," she said, brushing away tears. "Let's hurry down the approach and meet the kin."

For auld lang syne, my dear,
For auld lang syne,
We'll take a cup of kindness yet
For auld lang syne.

Robert Burns

SIX

The driveway veered left following a shallow ravine and opened into a vast complex of outbuildings and barns. Earlier, the buildings had shielded the true number of kinsmen from their view. Now, much to their surprise, they discovered over two hundred of the clan had lingered in the shadows. As they approached the largest of the barns, spontaneous cheers erupted as did songs and clapping. Reawakened into sober revelry, the kilted men began charging at Old Rover as though the passengers inside designated dignitaries or rock stars.

Most of the clansmen dressed alike in traditional family colors. Leather whisky-laden sporran purses draped the front of their kilts with most of the purse whisky already consumed. The women dressed in longer tartan skirts and long-sleeved white blouses. Some of the younger and more liberated lassies dared to wear wee-short male kilts. A bagpipe ensemble waited in the wings to perform 'little music' for the afternoon dancing. Three huge whiskey barrels sat on a makeshift wooden stage, tapped and readied for disemboweling; one had been emptied prematurely. A sign draped across the largest of the three barns read 'Welcome Home Ye Bonnie Kinsmen.' With a reunion analogous to prodigal sons returning, the Texas branch of the MacLaren clan was being reunited in grand style.

As Old Rover coasted to a stop, the procession of applauding cousins and family swarmed the car. Wanting to be the first to greet Mary Catherine, Brother James drew open the car door,

"Dearest sister, it's been years since we've seen each other but now that you're here, it seems like it was just yesterday when I last held ya in my arms. You're as beautiful as I ever remember."

He kissed Mary Catherine on the cheek and helped her out. She struggled with the first step but managed to limp to the stage with his arm wrapped securely around her waist. Cappy and the boys followed James' lead. They waved to the group of rowdy relatives, politely tipping their hats to the well-wishers, mothers and children. Once they assembled on the stage, the five honorees sat while James, the clan thane, staggered to the podium for a long overdue speech.

"Now we may have started a little early on the drinkin', but it was only because we got so excited about Mary Catherine finally comin' home. Hell," he piped in a rousing fashion, "that's what partying ceilidhs are for anyway. Drinkin'."

A cheer went up from the clan, most of whom had never seen the lost sister, let alone real cowboys from Texas.

"Not only has Mary Catherine come home," James continued, "but she's brought her loving husband, Cappy, her two grandsons, Little Nate and Steven, and her adopted son, Emilio. Let's hear a round of applause for them all."

On that note, James decided it best to wait for the cheers and clapping to subside.

"Now, we know Mary Catherine is ill, so let's not pretend it's a secret. We all know Cappy sold his Texas ranch to bring her back home and save this wonderful place of ours. They believed so much in Haddington Moor that they sunk every last pound to their names in this farm. That took a lot of courage—" The relatives' applause interrupted him mid-sentence and he 'shushed' them quiet. "And it also took courage for you young lads to come over here, take a chance, and help Cappy and Mary Catherine. We're all proud of you and proud MacLaren blood is in your veins."

This time the applause drowned out his words.

"*Speak up James. We can't hear ya,*" one of the cousins shouted.

"Ha. Right back at ya, cousin. Now, let me finish here and I'll be on me way. As I was sayin', we're all so very thankful that five hundred head of cattle ready are sitting on the Pier of Leith and ready to be trucked in on Tuesday afternoon, one full day ahead of our midnight deadline with the bank. Let's hear a round of applause for our heroes."

While applause got unleashed, Cappy stood and whispered something in James' ear and sat back down.

"Well, I stand corrected, clan brothers and sisters. The count is five hundred and one with the arrival today of a new calf. So, as I was sayin', it looks as though Haddington Moor will indeed remain in the family because of the generosity and sacrifice of the people you see before you. Now, the first order of business is to present the colors to each of our family members. Will granddaughter Katy please hand out our tartan sashes?"

Katy MacLaren, age sixteen, was one of the kilt-clad lassies whose short skirt and proud legs attracted Nate's attention early on. Nate's inquisitive eyes fixated on the attractive buxom cousin. As she passed in front of him, curtsied and handed him a sash, he couldn't help but wonder if second cousins were off limits. Keep your mind off the girl, he told himself, but when she bowed before him, her cleavage revealed a well-endowed figure. That's when the other inner voice seized command of his thoughts. Any hint of a conscience from Nathaniel Sterling became more of a knee-jerk reaction to the "respectability and manners" his grandmother had attempted to instill. Thus, behaving as he would with any young lady he fancied, he winked at Katy. To his amazement, she winked back.

"Now that the colors have been presented," continued James, "I propose a toast. Everyone grab a dram and raise your glasses on high: To my dearest sister, Mary Catherine, for loving Haddington Moor as much as life itself. To Cappy, for bringing home the Texas clan and sacrificing so much. To Steven, Emilio, and Little Nate, for putting family above their own self-interests. And to all the MacLarens past and present, the best damned clan in the Lothians."

"HERE. HERE." The family shouted.

On cue, the bagpipers, all elderly cousins, emerged from the barn and began pumping their leather satchels for the musical performance. The humid weather and heavy drinking, however, inhibited their abilities to inflate the bags. The fact none of the band members appeared under age eighty might also have had something to do with their inability to perform.

"We just can't get it up, James," Cousin Edward complained.

"Don't worry about it, boys. I've had the problem once or twice meself," James replied with a wide toothy smirk. "Look boys, we've still got the fiddles and the drums to march us to the little music," he continued. "While the music is a-playin', let's all introduce ourselves to these fine people."

With his eldest son, Angus, in tow, he began the long formalities. The others lined up by the stage, eager to shake hands and meet the Texas family. Of them all, however, Angus was the least happy over their arrival.

Angus MacLaren had struggled with the custodianship of the farm from the very first day he inherited it. When his mother died eight years earlier, his father, James, lost the appetite for farming and turned over the reins—perhaps, prematurely. Considered an honor, the custodian managed the last vestige of property still uniting the widely dispersed clan. Angus lived in the 'big house' with wife, Elizabeth (her second marriage), and daughter, Katy; stepdaughter, Heather, had moved out years before to attend the university.

While a decent fellow, Angus had always been short on business sense and was thoroughly unprepared to manage the complexities of a cattle operation. In spite of some fair performances before the mad cow epidemic, not a single steer remained on the pastures of Haddington Moor; all were slaughtered due to the mad cow disease. For the past year, he had struggled financially. For weeks, his family survived solely on the money Cappy wired. Even inept Angus realized a non-operational cattle facility could not withstand an unyielding bank. The deadline on Wednesday loomed dangerously too close for comfort. Yet, rather than revel in the reuniting of families and last minute heroics of his American aunt and uncle, he resented the bailout.

"So, Steven, from your grandmother's letters, I read how you received a degree in agricultural studies," Heather remarked as she worked her way down the stage.

"That's right. I got it about three years ago."

"Well, your grandmother says the past two years you've been able to show a profit. That has to be quite an accomplishment."

"It's really no different than any business. Mainly, you have to know what you're doing. If you control your costs, assuming the bottom hasn't fallen out of the market, you can make money. With all this fertile land you have here at Haddington Moor, if you grow the right kind of grasses, you can minimize feed costs. The drawback is you might not be able to support the number of head you've historically run because of the time needed to grow and rotate crops. . . ."

As he continued speaking, she sensed he knew the cattle business. "We obviously could have used you long ago. Nobody here knows what *he's* doing," she stated loudly enough for Angus to hear. The ploy worked. Angus stomped off the stage muttering drunken obscenities over a shoulder.

"I didn't realize you were living out here, too," Steven replied, oblivious to her earlier snide remark.

"No, I'm not—or can't. Or didn't you know? It's against clan rules for unmarried non-MacLarens over twenty-one years of age to live here. Then again, it really doesn't matter. I've got a flat in Edinburgh where I'm finishing up studies at the university in political science."

"Sounds fascinating. I've always loved anything dealing with politics. What are you going to—"

"Excuse me, Steven," Heather interrupted. "I'm supposed to be keeping an eye on my hormonally active half-sister, Katy. It appears she's got the hot flashes for your cousin. I'm afraid I'd better go rescue the dear lad before the siren sweeps him away."

Steven grabbed Heather's hand and repositioned himself directly in front of her beeline. "Oh, no, you don't. Little Nate's a big boy and can take care of himself. If your sister is all you say she is, she'll have her hands full. Trust me."

"Well, she is a bit, how would you say—*hyper*."

Stephen chuckled. "Sounds like a match made in heaven. Tell you what, Heather. Let's you and I go for a walk and you can show me around this farm. I'm not much into bagpipes and drums."

"That sounds like a marvelous idea," she replied, interlocking her arm with his. "I don't care for it at all that much either. I'm more of a Garth Brooks and U2 fan myself."

"That's pretty remarkable," he added. "So am I."

"And do you have a girlfriend back in Texas, Little Nate?" Katy teased.

"Sure. Don't I look like the kind of fella that would have a girlfriend?"

"Aye. Just judging from those strong broad shoulders and that smart cowboy hat, I'd say you had a girl every day of the week," she said, teasing his male ego.

"Not everyday, Katy. A fella has got to rest up once in awhile." Nate bragged, hamming it up while batting his eyelashes.

"Well, when I first saw you up here on the stage, I said to myself, 'Now there's a lad who doesn't need any rest. Who can probably ride those wild Texas ponies all day long if he has to.'"

"Actually, Katy, I've been known to ride a few fillies all night long, over and over and over, if you catch my drift," he said, puffing up his chest.

"So, answer this for me Mr. Endurance: Why do they call ya *Little* Nate?"

By now, he decided that he had either met his match or was peering into the dark eyes of a kilted she-devil in Scotland.

"Tell you what," Nate answered with a not so subtle wink. "I'll tell you why they call me *Little* if you'll let me see what's under the kilt."

"That's a deal," Katy chirped. She grabbed his hand and led him into the smallest of the three barns, the one used for storing grain and bales, and locked the door behind them. She hoisted herself on the tall stacking table with her legs dangling over its edge. He quickly moved in front with his stomach pressed against her knees.

"You go first, cowboy. Why do they call you *Little*?"

"Because when I was a small boy, before they put me on

Ritalin, my mother kept calling me the 'Little Monster.' Grandpa didn't like her calling me that so he started calling me 'Little Nate.' It just stuck all these years. That's all there is to it. Now it's your turn, Katy. What's under the kilt?"

"Well, Little Nate, how would you like to see the locks of Scotland?"

Nate's face contorted. "Why the heck would I want to see the lochs of Scotland? It's just a bunch of water—a friggin' lake or something."

"Not the 'lochs,' silly—I'm talking about the curly locks of Katy MacLaren," she whispered while raising her skirt and spreading her legs apart.

In most amorous situations Nate rarely exhibited self-control. Still, he knew better than to pursue the offer. He placed his hands on Katy's knees and kilt, keeping her from exposing what surely would have been temptation beyond his power. "Cousin, where are your manners? Your respectability?" he asked with a deadpan stare. "Katy, maybe I gave you the wrong impression about me. I'm just a humble cowboy looking for a good time. And you're my cousin, for Pete's sake—"

"Second cousin." She corrected.

"Fine. Second cousin. Either way, we're family. Tell you what. Instead of us staying all cooped up inside this here barn, how would you like to dance with the *Lock's Nest Monster*?"

She giggled. "You're a funny one, Little Nate. Sure. Why not? Let's dance."

"Good. You can teach me how to do a jig to that fiddling outside you call music." He pulled her toward the door, this time seizing her by the hand and seizing the lead.

"Aye. I'll teach you to dance. That I will, cowboy."

By the time Emilio repaired the tractor's split vacuum line, Angus had brought him a cold stout and a rag to clean up.

"I didn't mean to pull you away from the ceilidh like that, young man."

"Oh, it was my pleasure to help. I've always loved working with my hands, especially ancient Ford engines. My uncle has one like this down in the Valley, so I knew what the problem was as soon as you described the symptoms."

"Well, we're lucky to have you here, lad, else she'd be a-sittin' there lettin' the weeds grow through her cracks."

Emilio pondered their situation as he gazed upon the fields. "Once we get the cattle here, Angus, we're going to need this tractor of yours operational. Steven has a real good method of shredding manure and using it as a natural fertilizer when we rotate the herds through pastures. This old tractor will come in real handy. Sure beats spreading it by hand."

"Aye. Good for you smart lads. So smart at this business you all are. So, tell me, are you as good with the whip as you've been boastin' to the cousins? The rumor is you're so dexterous you could herd a Frenchman to a bidet."

"I've been known to swat horse flies at fifteen feet."

"Fifteen feet? You don't say? Now this I've got to see. In fact, it's something we should all see." Angus hurriedly gathered some of the family members into a circle while Emilio retrieved the bullwhip. When Emilio returned to the main barn a few minutes later, Angus had already placed a cigarette in his mouth and challenged the cowboy to split it in half.

"Come on now, lad. Don't disappoint the family. After all, you Texans are supposed to be so good at everything. Let's see if you can live up to all the advertising."

Induced by drink, Angus' glib tongue overshadowed his normally reticent demeanor. Fortunately, Cappy appeared on the scene before any damage could be done.

"What on earth is going on here, son?" he asked.

"Angus wants me to show everyone how good I am with the whip." Then, in a softer voice, he added, "I may have bragged a little too much, Cappy."

"Oh, is that what it was—braggin'?" Angus countered. "I thought everything was naturally bigger and better in Texas. Like profitable farms. Land like milk and honey that miraculously gives birth to calves after six months in the wilds. Or maybe you've just been spreading too much of that recycled manure around?"

By now, the rest of the clan heard the commotion and gathered full force.

"So, what is it lad?" Angus continued, twirling so everyone could hear his challenge. "You don't have the balls to do it? Or, should I say, don't have the *huevos?*"

The ethnic slur enraged Emilio. "I'll show you, *bandejo,*" he mumbled. Eager to face the challenge, he laid the tail of the whip flat on the ground and measured the exact distance to Angus. He instructed Angus to turn sideways and clamp down on the cigarette. By the time Angus nodded his head and signaled ready, the tail had already cracked and exploded with a concussion that disintegrated the cigarette. A roar of approval went up from the clan. The cousins hoisted Emilio on their shoulders and paraded him around the stage. For the rest of the afternoon the young Tejano was the toast of Haddington Moor. "To the amazing bullwhip master," they chanted before tossing back drams of whiskey.

Angus, retreated to the safer confines of the big house where he spent the remainder of the day in a deep whisky sleep with visions of infallible Texans tormenting his slumber.

By 10:30PM the sun had crept behind the hills and Mary Catherine was feeling exhausted by the day's events. With Cappy by her side, she retired to the bothy, the thatched roof cottage that would become their living quarters. Off in the

distance, Steven and Heather walked the high meadow while
Pedo scampered by their side. Emilio, a dozen drams to the
wind, had developed a brogue. Little Nate and Katy danced
as cousins clapped to the Texan's unorthodox jig, all as the
music of the fiddles and the laughter of the intoxicated
dancers echoed off the walls of White Castle Fortress a mile
away.

It was a day to remember at Haddington Moor—the day
the clan reunited as a family.

The golden hours on angels' wings,
Flew over me and my dearie;
For dear to me as light and life,
Was my sweet Highland Mary.

Robert Burns

<u>*SEVEN*</u>

Cappy comforted Mary Catherine most of the night. Her vomiting had finally subsided and she was asleep again but he was not—he could not. Holding her in his arms, he knew every day from now on would be a struggle Every hour would be weighed heavily on angels' wings. She had held on the past few days to glimpse Haddington Moor one last time. She had willed herself to live long enough to see her boys embrace their birthright. Now with the family together, she was at peace and her will to live had diminished; life seemed of secondary importance. To complicate matters, Cappy was unable to help her endure the pain. He asked her to give him more time and to be stronger for a few more days. He told her he simply could not bear life without her by his side. "Do not leave me," he pleaded. She whispered she would try her best to delay the inevitable before falling asleep in his arms.

As she lay in bed, he gently stroked her head and began what would become the long grieving process. He recalled the years they had spent together, raising their children in West Texas and the episodes with her behind the wheel of Old Rover. He missed Texas something fierce, he told himself, but he would miss her much more.

Then, after what seemed liked hours, he began to stir from melancholy to euphoria, for he had devised what he considered an ingenious plan. He knew exactly what it would take to get Mary Catherine through another day. He would worry about the following day when that day dawned.

The boys had been bunking and asleep in the attic in the big house when James came calling on Mary Catherine and Cappy. He rapped on the bothy's front door.

"Mornin'. Don't tell me everybody's asleep in there, too, on this beautiful Sunday mor-r-rnin'?" he asked, singing his best Lothian brogue. "I thought for sure the boys would be up but they're as fast asleep as calves in a manger. Too bad for them. Offhand, I'd say this is one of the finest days I've seen in quite some time. Why, it's full of God's gr-r-race and hope. It'd be a real shame to waste it on slumber."

"Morning back to you, James. Yes, we're definitely awake in here. I'm just helping Mary Catherine get dressed."

"Well, I won't be comin' in. I just thought I'd see if you'd like to go to town with me."

"That's awfully nice of you but we've got other plans today."

"Oh, ya do, do ya? And what might they be?"

"I can't tell you in front of Mary Catherine. It's a secret."

"A secret it will stay, Cappy. You two go and have a good time. But, as long as I'm here thinkin' on it, what time are you leavin' tomorrow mornin' to sign the release papers at Customs? I wanted Angus to be there with ya."

"How about 8:00?"

"Sounds good. I'll let the lad know."

After the previous night's stunt, Cappy wasn't sure if he wanted Angus along for the company. It was obvious his nephew held deep-rooted hostility for the Sterlings. He hoped time would eventually heal wounds fueled by pride and ego. Still, recalling the confrontation between Angus and Emilio, Cappy couldn't help but snort in disgust over the incident.

"What's wrong, dearest?" Mary Catherine asked.

"Nothing. Nothing at all. Let's hurry up and leave. I have big plans for us today."

As he helped her out the cottage and along the back porch, she asked him to stop for a moment. Peering to the northwest and less than a hundred yards away, she could see Drum Ridge and the rye meadow where she picked wildflowers as a child.

"Cappy, see that small ridge over there? The one laden with the rye grass?" she asked, pointing to the spot that for many years had yielded flowers. "Later today could you pick me some pink twinflowers? They're usually in full bloom by now."

"Of course, I can," he answered. "Of course, I can."

He led her to the Defender and opened her door. She grabbed the mackerel bar as he lifted her onto the seat and, with his help, swung her legs around to the front. Behind her, she spied the picnic basket he prepared earlier. And, behind the picnic basket propped two caged roadrunners. She smiled and waved to Sir Charles.

"You never did tell me where we were going this morning, Cappy, and why Sir Charles and Camilla are riding with us."

"You'll see, Miss Mary. Just hold your horses. You'll see. Right now, I'm doing good just to figure out how to drive this contraption."

Cappy started the engine and for only the second time in his life found himself sitting behind the steering wheel of Old Rover. He cautiously threw it into first gear, eased out on the clutch and, without any hint of resistance, the jalopy inched forward. Cappy smiled. "I'll be," he whispered. "That was easier than I remember."

They drove for nearly a half-mile along the rutted road leading southwest from the farmhouse and barns to the back pastures. Once in the clearing, he made an abrupt left on the incline leading up a steep hill.

"Where in the world are you taking me, Cappy. Certainly not up to that craggy auld lookout?"

He remained reticent while concentrating on his driving technique. Once the Defender shifted into four-wheel drive, the rest of the forty-degree grade to the summit surrendered in less than five minutes. When they reached the top, the panoramic view was breathtaking. To the northeast towered Berwick Law, just as Mary Catherine had said. To the south lay the ridge of hills leading to the Lammermuir range. Grassy meadows with endless wildflowers stretched forever beyond the horizon in all directions.

"This is it," he whispered excitedly. "This is really it." Pleased with himself, he turned to face her and gaze into her eyes. "I'm told if you can see Berwick Law from this spot, it means the weather will be good and the day will be long."

She reached out and touched his cheek. Exhausted from the ordeals of illness, she still had the strength to recognize his devotion. "You sweet, sweet man. How ever did you know this was my secret place?"

"Miss Mary, for over fifty years I've been listening to you tell me about it. As we were driving in yesterday, I knew in an instant this had to be the place. So, today you and I are going to have a picnic up here. After all, you promised me the first day we met that you'd share it with me."

"Aye, that I did," she affirmed, still touching his cheek. "And you, dearest, have indeed fulfilled your two promises to me. I love you so very much."

He kissed her on the forehead and opened the car door. Before attending to Mary Catherine, he removed the fragile contents of the Defender's cargo hold and, after a few minutes, came back and assisted her out of the vehicle. He laid her on the blanket that had already spread on the ground, and positioned her north where the warm late morning breeze patted her face. Next, he apportioned cheese and crackers on her family china, and opened a bottle of wine and poured her a glass. They didn't say much at first but simply held each other's hands and relished the view and the breeze. Cappy watched her nostrils flare as she soaked in the aromas that basked memories. He sensed she had not forgotten the intoxicating fragrance or the days of her youth from this very perch.

"So, is this where you plan on releasing Sir Charles and Camilla?" she finally asked, breaking the long silence.

"Yes—yes it is," he answered.

"I can't think of a more fitting spot in all Scotland," she said, attempting to break a smile.

"Nor I, Miss Mary."

He stood and walked to the grassy knoll where the cage sat. Unlatching the wire gate, he flung its door open. At first, the two roadrunners were hesitant to leave the nest where they had been jailed for nearly a month but, soon enough, the overpowering urge for freedom proved too much—that and the sunflower seeds Cappy laid three feet away. Like most good mates, Camilla watched as Sir Charles gorged himself on the tasty tidbits. When there was nothing left, the birds simply bobbed their heads and scurried off with Camilla taking up a rear pursuit.

"Do you think they understand?" Mary Catherine asked as the birds departed from sight.

"As much as any of us," Cappy replied.

Mary Catherine abruptly cocked her head to listen to a distant rustling originating from the big house, off in the distance. Her eyes strained watching human activity stir on the farm. "That almost looks like Steven and Heather down there, doesn't it?"

"Actually, it is. I think Steven's found himself a

girlfriend."

"That's a good thing, Cappy. She'd be darned lucky to have a fine young man like our Steven—"

"And he her," Cappy interrupted.

"So much like you and me they are."

"There's no one like you, Miss Mary," he said, kissing her again on the forehead. "How 'bout I read you some poetry from our friend Robert B.?"

"Oh, would you, Cappy? That's such a smart idea."

He reached inside the picnic basket, pulled out their favorite book and read aloud:

> "She is a winsome wee thing,
> She is a handsome wee thing,
> She is a lonesome wee thing,
> This sweet wee wife of mine,
>
> I never saw a fairer,
> I never loved a dearer,
> And near my heart I'll wear her,
> For fear my jewel tine.
>
> She is a winsome wee thing,
> She is a handsome wee thing,
> She is a lonesome wee thing,
> This dear wee wife of mine.
>
> The world's wrack we share of it,
> The warstle and the care of it;
> With her I'll blythely bear it,
> And think my lot divine."

Mary Catherine squeezed his hand again. "That one is nice, dearest husband. Now, I have a stanza I would like to read to you:

"All hail, ye tender feelings dear.
The smile of love, the friendly tear.
The Sympathetic glow.
Long since, this world's thorny ways
Had numbered out my weary days,
Had it not been for you.
Fate still has blest me with a friend,
In every care and ill. . . ."

They read to each other for hours, lost in the common passion for the poetry of the farm boy named Robert from Ayrshire.

By mid-afternoon, the intense rays forced him to tie a bonnet on her head to shield her eyes from the sun. He put on his cowboy hat for the same reason. Sensing she was growing tired of the poetry, he reached inside the picnic basket again, this time pulling out the portable tape player belonging to Little Nate.

"My word, Cappy." she exclaimed. "First it's Robert Burns' book. Next, it's Nathaniel's boom box. What other secret delights do you have in that basket?"

"Just the tape player," he answered, fumbling with the loader while inserting their favorite cassette. "Little Nate loaned it to me."

Within seconds, Glen Miller's *Moonlight Serenade* echoed down the heather valley of Haddington Moor, past the scattering of buildings and out beyond Drum Ridge. Cappy wasted no time. He stood and bowed slightly at the hips. "May I have this dance?" he asked.

Mary Catherine looked up at him and gave a coy wink. "I'll give it all I've got, cowboy."

He lifted her into his arms. She laid her head against his shoulder, and they relived their first dance in London to the same unmistakable song—the same song where midway through the refrain he kissed her; the same song they later made love to while the air raid sirens wailed. It was at that moment in time, so many years before, when they both knew they could never be apart. Reluctantly, they danced a last dance, lost in memories from high on the lookout overlooking the pink twinflowers. And at that moment in time, there was an unspoken silence between them as they embraced on the hill she claimed as her secret place, as they savored one more day basking in the sunlight together.

In Edinburgh town they've made a law,
In Edinburgh at the Court of Sessions,
That standing pricks are faulted all,
And guilty of high transgressions.

Robert Burns

EIGHT

"Minister Sessions, will this affect all U.S. beef imports?" the reporter shouted the question from the rear as she elbowed her way through the packed gathering.

The minister glared at the young woman as she squirmed forward and thrust a microphone in his face. He disdained over zealous reporters, especially neophytes out to establish a name for themselves. Ironically, if anyone knew about over zealous ambition, he did, and she reeked of the stuff.

"Holly Gunter with the World News Network, sir. Does the Agricultural Minister care to comment further on whether the cattle embargo announced this morning will affect all U.S. livestock, livestock we know to be immune to Mad Cow Disease?"

"The embargo will affect every nation's livestock," he answered coolly, still smiling at the news cameras. After posing a few seconds longer for still camera shots, he lowered his voice and turned to face Holly head-on. "So, tell me, Miss. Why is it you Yanks keep referring to Bovine Spongiform Encephalopathy as Mad Cow Disease? At least have the wherewithal to refer to the abbreviation—BSE."

The condescending tone set her off. Without thinking, she fired back. "Excuse me, Minister Sessions, for my slip of the tongue." She curtsied in an exaggerated gentrified fashion. "Or, should I simply address you as *Your Highness?*"

A round of applause went up from the news people and bystanders who had assembled at the Edinburgh Customs House lower steps for the morning press conference. They did not care for the government's messenger, either. They, too, disliked the unilateral embargo Great Britain imposed on the world, but Her Majesty's minister had seen fit to shut down the port to all livestock trade, both in and out of the country. Three confirmed deaths from CJD, the human equivalent of 'Mad Cow,' had just been confirmed.

"Miss Gunter, while I do realize the move is not popular with your current administration or your cattle lobbyists, let me state for the record that the safety of the British public comes first," he chided, taking advantage of what he assumed would become positive media spin. He abruptly raised his voice and pontificated, wagging a finger in her face. "Even above the interests of America," he added. *Camera flash. Camera flash.*

Duped into the confrontation, Holly fired off a second salvo. "Is it the safety of the British public you're seeking, sir, or how best to position yourself for becoming the next Prime Minister?"

The other reporters and the angry U.K. National Cattle Association members gasped upon hearing the question. For a few uncomfortable seconds, an eerie hush swept over the gathering; all eyes affixed on Holly.

"Miss Gunter, or whatever your sniveling little name is, you must have just stepped off a cattle boat yourself and obviously don't understand how things work on this side of the pond. I'll ignore that comment of yours for now and trust your Atlanta office will do a much better job selecting their *next* U.K. correspondent." His face contorted holding back rage. He abruptly looked past her to the other reporters. "Anyone else care to give it a go?"

Stunned by the rebuttal, Holly recoiled. Thoughts of a once promising career in journalism began to dissipate. She messed up again, she told herself. *Big time*. Philip, her boss, would be furious. In the past twelve months, he had assigned her three new jobs, each a result of her tongue wagging at the wrong time. This was supposed to be her last hurrah. Meanwhile, other reporters eager to field respectful questions, pushed past her. As Holly Gunter and her cameraman, George, retreated up the stairway and away from the vultures encircling the Agricultural Minister, she couldn't help but get in one last jab. "*F#*king* prick," she yelled from the top step. Yet, between the vociferous mob of reporters, the heckling of protesters, and the everyday street traffic, no one heard her off-the-cuff taunt.

The sixth child and only daughter of Robert and Edna Gunter, Holly mastered the harsher vocabulary of the male species early in life. When at the tender age of eight, her parents died in a fiery automobile accident, oldest brother, Joseph, a fisherman twenty years her senior, became by default the surrogate head of household. The fact Joseph never married and remained devout to his patriarchal role never got questioned. Such was the curse and responsibility of the eldest, for the lad took his job in earnest by making sure his baby sister, the "brains of the family," was never waylaid into the business of lobster fishing like the rest of the family. Thus, it became Joseph's personal quest to make sure Holly got out of Massachusetts and into a respectable vocation.

Sure enough, one-by-one the brothers worked the trade, trapping lobster off the coast of Marblehead and the rich banks and shoals that had sustained the family since the mid-1800s. And, while nuns tutored Holly during the day at nearby *Her Lady of Piety*, the evening dinner table became the child's most impressionable education. Each meal systematically eradicated everything the sisters tried beating into her hell-bent head. Soaking in the banter and salty language of the brothers, Holly preferred assimilating the idiom of the family.

"Anyone know why Beaners say *f#*king* so much?" she asked at age ten. Blank stares and shrugs reflected around the dinner table. "Because in kindergarten, they're taught the Beaner alphabet—*f#*king*-A, *f#*king*-B, *f#*king*-C. . . ."

Rousing laughter abounded, encouraging her trench mouth frivolity. Thus, over time, Holly grew conditioned to anything but piety. Secretly, she desired to be one of the boys. Nevertheless, one discernible quality stuck as she matured—the art of storytelling. By her senior year in high school, she managed to become the chief editor of the school newspaper, winning statewide competitions usually reserved for the more wholesome girls from respectable neighborhoods in Waban and Wesley.

Even after the family fell on hard times and lost the trawler to the Internal Revenue Service, the brothers managed to take up odd jobs in Marblehead and pool their incomes to send Holly south to Emory University in Atlanta. "Just fight the IRS bastards," she screamed at Joseph. "They can't steal our family's business. No *f#*king* way." But Joseph and the brothers voted against such a move for they knew they had profited illegally at the docks in cash trades; now they needed to pay the piper with the only lien-free asset to their name. It was the first of many assets the government would attempt to seize.

As their financial woes grew worse, Holly was forced to supplement the diminished monthly stipends from home with part-time work. Eventually, she enrolled in the co-op journalism program at Emory, plying a semester at WNN and another on-campus. During that first interview with the

World News Network, asked why the prestigious news organization should hire her, a mere B- student, as an intern, she answered with a straight-face, stretching the truth a tad, "Because my mother's brother, Ted Tillson, once told me there was no fairer craft in the world than that of broadcast journalism." Never mind that the founder and owner of WNN was not remotely related. The fact Uncle Ted's name instilled fear in all underlings prompted swift employment. Not even the WNN human resources team bothered to check the validity of the yarn. Holly was that believable.

Three years into her co-op education, Holly realized the truth would soon be discovered and she 'd be snared in the lie as easily as lobster in one of her brothers' cages. She reasoned that if she could just get established in the craft before doomsday struck, a job with another network such as CNN would avail itself. Out of necessity, she sucked-up to her boss, Philip, doing all the necessary things to get the highly touted assignment in London.

Now, disgraced in London, she was having second thoughts about the deception, about honesty, and about all the good virtues the nuns tried vainly to instill. She longed for Massachusetts and missed that "old-coot-slave-driver," Philip Robenowitz.

The two mystery men carefully skirted the press conference and the two reporters parked on the top steps of the Customs House, and slid through the front doors unnoticed—except by Holly who was savoring a cigarette while mocking the reporters below. Always maintaining an observant eye for a potential news story, Holly turned to her cameraman for an assessment. "George, anything look peculiar about this picture?" She asked the question framing the two men inside her box-shaped thumbs and index fingers for George's perusal.

"Yeah. One is short; the other one is tall. One could stand

to lose a few pounds and the tall one is dressed *like a cowboy*. What in the world is a cowboy doing in Scotland?"

"My thoughts exactly. Come on. Let's find out."

"Holly, we're going to get in trouble with Philip if we leave. We're supposed to cover this briefing."

"Come on, George. Come on. This one smells like a real story. A real human interest story. The kind we like but never get assigned." She coaxed George along, tugging his arm. "Come on."

"But we're going to miss the briefing and—"

"Damn it, George. They're getting away," she interrupted. "*F#*k* the briefing."

With that, the cub reporter and her cameraman chased after the strangers, spying as the two men rounded a corner; sprinting and scurrying behind the next corner until the men vanished again from sight. When Cappy and Angus ultimately strolled under a sign marked 'Livestock and Animal Documentation Centre,' Holly instructed George to conceal his camera. Then, they crept through the door and quietly observed from a distance.

"May I help you, sirs?" A well-manicured civil servant peered upward from behind the counter. His voice squeaked asking the question.

"Yes, you may," Cappy replied. "I'm here to get my paperwork stamped so I can clear out my cattle. We've got over five hundred head quarantined in your pens. Made arrangements to have 'em shipped out this afternoon, and—"

"Excuse me, sir—*excuse me*," the clerk blurted out. "Your cattle can't be released."

Cappy's face twisted in bewilderment.

"You apparently don't understand the situation," the man continued. "The Minister of Agriculture has quarantined all cattle imports as of this morning."

"Well, I guess you don't understand. We've had our cattle here since Saturday. If this quarantine went into effect this morning, it doesn't apply to our herd."

"I'm sorry, sir, but you're not the only one affected by this."

"Listen to me, you wet-behind-the-ears mama's boy, those are Texas cattle we're talking about and Texas cattle don't have that disease. I've got a deadline to meet. I've got a farm the bank is ready to put under if I don't deliver that herd in two days, and I've made a promise to my wife and her family. By God, you don't ever want to come between me and my word."

George's camera silently rolled capturing the heated exchange of words.

"Well, sir, you won't be keeping your word today."

"And just who is going to stop me?"

"Minister Sessions, sir. He's our nation's agricultural head of state."

"Then, who in blue blazes is his boss?"

"That would be the P.M.—the Prime Minister."

By now, Angus had determined the odds of winning this debate stacked too heavily against them. He leaned over and whispered, "Cappy, let it go. There's nothing we can do. This thing is much bigger than us. It's r-rooted in hysteria and you can't fight that, man. You can't fight it."

"*Yes, you can*," Holly burst out. "I'm sorry. I—we didn't mean to interrupt. I'm Holly Gunter with WNN and this is my camera operator, George. We followed you here because, well, frankly, you don't see a cowboy in Scotland everyday. And I had a hunch about you two men."

"How's that, Miss Gunter?" Cappy asked, somewhat confused by her presence.

"Listen to me, cowboy. You don't know these bastards like I do. The only way you're going to beat them is with the kind of exposure WNN provides. If you'll give me first coverage rights to this story, I can promise you we'll make these worms squirm. But, even if you don't want my help, don't give up. Whatever you do, don't give up the fight."

"I don't plan on giving up, Miss Gunter. And with an attitude like yours on our side, you bet WNN can have the coverage rights."

"That's great, Cappy. It's Cappy, right?"

"John David Sterling of Texas," he responded, tipping his hat. "They call me 'Cappy.' This here is my nephew, Angus MacLaren, the custodian of Haddington Moor, a cattle farm in the Lothians. As I was saying, let me assure you and anyone watching me through that camera lens of yours, we're going to get our cattle to Haddington Moor one way or another."

"That's the spirit, Cappy," she said, slugging him on the shoulder. She hurriedly repositioned herself in front of him, holding the microphone to her mouth, and pointed to her cameraman. "*Roll it, George*—This is Holly Gunter from inside Edinburgh Customs House. I'm here this morning with one of the first casualties of the British government's indiscriminate cattle embargo. I'm here with Texas rancher John David Sterling and his Scottish nephew, Angus MacLaren. . . ."

When Holly finished the narrative, she turned the microphone toward the elderly cowboy and, for a few heartfelt minutes, Cappy told his story. He told of his dying wife, about selling their ranch in Texas to rescue the land she loved in Scotland, and how the family's future depended on this herd for survival. His speech prompted one last question from Holly.

"And just how far do you intend to take your fight, Mr. Sterling?"

Cappy hesitated before answering. Recalling the run-in with the Port of Houston Authority years earlier, this escapade seemed all too familiar. Why does this always happen to me? To us? he thought. Yet, he knew there was still only one right answer. "How far? I'll tell you how far,

Miss Gunter: All the way to Jesus Christ, Himself, if I have to."

"Cut," she yelled to George. "That's a wrap. Perfect, Cappy. Absolutely perfect."

"Man, this is gonna win you a Pulitzer or something," George whispered.

"Screw the Pulitzer, George. Let's just get the man his cattle."

Holly grabbed Cappy by the arm and dragged him down the hallway, running and yanking him out the main door of the Customs House and bypassing the news conference still in progress.

"Where ar-r-re we going, Miss Gunter?" Angus panted, trying to keep pace.

"To Number Ten Downing Street—the residence of Jesus Christ."

The Fight

The eagle from the cliffy brow,
Marking you his prey below,
In his breast no pity dwells,
Strong necessity compels.

Robert Burns

NINE

Even before they reached the train station, George had already downloaded Holly's story to his computer. Using the laptop, he re-edited the verbal confrontation between Cappy and the customs agent and, with the push of a button, transferred the data via the new cellular modem hookup to Atlanta (all this being the latest technology in 1996). Seconds later, their producer received the same images and Holly scrambled to explain why this isolated event took precedent over the briefing televised by rival CNN.

"Look, Philip, I'm not arguing with you anymore. Just, just quit yelling—Yes, uh-huh, uh-huh, no, no-o-o. Now quit yelling. You're going to have another heart attack. I'm not going to be a party to this—I'm simply going to hang up. Here it goes. I'm hanging up—You look at what I sent you and call me back—I'm hanging up. Love you. Bye."

Cappy, not knowing quite what to make of the fragmented one-sided telephone conversation, took his cowboy hat off and laid it on the train seat. "Everything go okay with your boss in Atlanta, Miss Gunter?"

"Oh, that?" She sighed. "It went fine. Wouldn't you

agree, George?"

George smiled guiltily and flashed an 'OK' hand gesture.

"See. Even George thinks it went fine. And, you don't need to keep calling me 'Miss Gunter.' Since we're going to be spending a lot of time together over the next few days, just call me Holly."

"All right, Miss Holly—"

"No, not 'Miss Holly,' just *Holly*," she said, patting Cappy on the knee. As she spoke those words, she noticed his gaunt face and how years of ranching in West Texas had weathered everything about him except his striking blue eyes. Wisps of thinned gray hair dangled over his eyebrows, obscuring liver spots and deep-set wrinkles on his forehead. As morning sunlight flooded through the train window, it finally occurred to her that the subject of her human-interest piece was frail—determined but very frail. Something other than physical stamina had to be driving him on this journey of theirs. "Never mind, Cappy. *Miss Holly* it is," she said, capitulating to the fact that he was probably too set in his ways to ever change his true nature.

"Well, what you said earlier about spending days together—I don't have days to fix this thing."

"I know you don't, Cappy. We'll just have to play with the cards we got dealt and hope for a miracle."

"Yes, Ma'am. I guess at this point, it would take a miracle."

"Or WNN," George interrupted, grinning with a devilish smirk.

In Atlanta, Philip Robenowitz felt his pulse for the second time, detecting what he feared would be the big one—a heart beat foretelling an impending attack or, worse, a stroke. His neurosis always conjured such things, especially when an epiphany struck. The last thing needed, he told himself, was to keel over on Holly's good fortune—a once in a lifetime news piece that could vault perennial second place WNN to the top. He definitely didn't need unchecked elation wasting him in his prime, at least not before retirement; at least not before CNN got kicked to hell and back in the ratings. Intuitively, he leaned back in his chair and puffed heavily on the Cuban cigar champed in his mouth. It was a tried and true relaxation technique learned years earlier. Nicotine had a way of weaving its magic and calming his senses. True, patience had never been one of his virtues and impatience played havoc with his heart, but today Holly's overwrought concern about his health would have to take a backseat to business.

"Damn it, I don't care if he is on the phone," Phillip suddenly blurted, turning to face his secretary. "Tell Don Prigmore to get in my office. *Now*."

Philip had already finished viewing Holly's interview and loved it. Now it was his boss's turn to give it the stamp of approval. He sneered at the thought—Don Prigmore needing to approve anything he did. What a useless wimp, Don Prigmore. The man was the latest in a long line of Yale bean counters who the top brass had forced upon him. Don Prigmore idled as another lazy executive stooge with no discernible talent for understanding the real nuts-and-bolts of how to make WNN number one.

For thirty years, Philip Robenowitz had been busting his tail in the television news racket, climbing the corporate ladder on an uncanny talent to recognize great stories and take abuse from bosses who didn't know their collective ways around the office water cooler. He blamed the "little ass-wipes" for hindering his creative style and for second-guessing him in the heat of battle. As a result, WNN always came in second place. Oh, how he hated second place. Worse, ratings determined salary and salary determined pension. All he needed was one singular high performance year as the managing producer of a first place news organization and he could retire. Just one good year and he could tell Don and all the rest of the Yale inbreeds to kiss his ever-loving rump goodbye.

Hung prominently on the wall behind his desk loomed a hand-tinted photograph of "baby," the 48-foot sloop anchored four hundred miles away at Boca Raton. Named *Pissonya II*, nobody really knew if there was ever a *Pissonya I* but, then again, nobody really knew Philip all that well. His X-style management persona forbade any mingling with fellow employees, that is, all except Holly who befriended him three years earlier while co-oping out of Emory. It was Holly who had confided in him the truth about how she and Ted Tillson were not really blood relatives. And, he loved her ruse. It reminded him of himself.

Afterhours, usually around 10:00PM and after the staff stampeded for the local watering hole, Holly and Philip stoked cigars in his office. Holly knew even more politically incorrect jokes than he did, and Holly could cuss with the best of the water cooler boys. In fact, Holly was the only one he had ever invited onboard "baby." They had even sailed the high seas together to the Grand Turk Islands the summer before. With three disastrous marriages and no children, Philip often stated that if could have ever produced a daughter, she no doubt would have been molded after Holly.

"Best damned piece I've seen in years, Edith," he screamed. "I knew our girl could do it. 'Knew it all the time."

Edith, his secretary, took whatever he said in stride. Her boss had won more broadcasting awards than the rest of the office combined. He simply had a nose for news. Yet, on this particular ditty, he seemed more self-assured; he flashed even more enthusiasm than the duped terrorist piece the British government set up the month before. That mistake mitigated a star reporter's firing and put his ass on the line. It also forced Holly's last second reassignment to London.

Phillip still frothed over the embarrassment. Indeed. Her boss was overdue for a big break, Edith told herself. In a show of support, she winked at him through their glass partition, flashing a thumbs-up sign of approval. He reciprocated grinning ear-to-ear.

"I want it run it at the bottom of the hour and every half hour segment after that. Understood? We're going to play this thing for all it's worth. And, I want that conference call with Holly and Dunlevy ready in ten minutes. Got it?"

Edith flashed another thumbs-up and buried her head in the telephone console, frantic to get all parties onboard.

For the past year Philip's handpicked protégée, Holly, had been a royal pain but today all the Tums and Pepcid tablets she'd induced him to take were paying off—that and the box of Cubans she'd sent overnight from London.

A minute later Don Prigmore stormed in Phillip's office.

"What in the world is so important, Philip? I was in the middle of a long distance call and—"

"Sit down, Don," Phillip barked back. "That call was just that high priced mistress of yours in Vegas. You don't think I know? I know everything that goes on around here. Now, shut up and pay attention. You need to approve this piece."

Philip clicked the play-file icon and the two men watched the interview on the oversized computer screen. When it finished Don jumped up, ecstatic.

"Wow. That's fantastic. So, where is Holly? She didn't let that old man get away, did she?"

"Hell, no. She's got him with her. In fact, they're taking the train to London as we speak—"

"I think we ought to play this for all it's worth," Don interjected. "You know. The big brother angle. How government makes heartless decisions that ruin people's lives. The little guy versus the bureaucracy. All that baloney." He paused to lean over Phillip's desk. His voice lowered as the thought struck. "Hey. It just dawned on me.

Why would the British government block our cattle exports when we don't have any cases of Mad Cow?"

"For Pete's sake, Don. What does have to do with anything? Who gives a shit?"

A blank look overtook Don. He shrugged. "Beats me."

"Sir," Edith hollered, rapping the partition glass, "I've got Mr. Dunlevy and Miss Gunter ready on the conference call."

Philip Robenowitz punched his speakerphone button and simultaneously connected the three parties:

> Dunlevy: "What's breaking, Philip and Don? It's 2:00AM here in LA, for crying out loud."
> Robenowitz: "We've got a story we want to run. 'Sort of a human-interest thing. Not what we normally do. We need your approval. If it's done right, we can really embarrass the British government. Make them look bad after they screwed us on that phony leak last month."
> Dunlevy: "Who's on it and what's the story line?"
> Gunter: "I'm on it, sir—Holly Gunter."
> Dunlevy: "Ted's niece? That Holly Gunter?"
> Gunter: "Y-y-yes, sir."
> Robenowitz: <light laughter>
> Dunlevy: "Well, hell. I'm awake now. You might as well drive the stake further in my heart. Tell me what's going down, Holly."
> Gunter: "Thank you, sir. I found this elderly Texas rancher in Edinburgh this morning while covering the embargo briefing. . . ."

Holly unfolded the story in detail for the three men. For ten minutes they listened to her tale, spellbound by her account of the struggling cowboy trying to make good his promise.

Gunter: ". . .and he and his nephew are with us. I thought we'd do a shoot in front of the Prime Minister's residence and see if we can get the Agriculture Ministry to back down. After all, his cattle should be exempt from the new policy."

Dunlevy: "Well, I feel bad for Mr. Sterling but sentiment in this business gets you nowhere. This piece of yours has got to boost ratings or there's no reason to run with it. And I sure as hell have to be able to justify it to the Board, especially if it bombs. Sounds compelling enough. It may be just the thing we need to attract the younger demographic. Can you guarantee me a two point increase over the next forty-eight hours?"

Robenowitz: "This is Philip, again. I can promise you *three* points. Maybe even the downfall of the British government on this boner of theirs."

Gunter: "We'll not only get you the points, Mr. Dunlevy, we'll also get you the head of that prick Sessions."

Dunlevy: "Holly, Philip—I don't give a rat's ass about toppling governments or decapitating arrogant assholes like Stephen Sessions. That's your agenda, not mine. The only thing I care about is kicking CNN's butt during this ratings period. So, run with it. Do whatever it takes to get me the points."

Prigmore: "Sir. This is Don Prigmore. We've already built a headline for it: *Captive Cattle Crisis in Scotland.* What do you think, sir?

Hello—Hello?"

The executive producer had already hung up and gone back to bed, no doubt to dream of the day when his network would rule the coveted ratings wars in the highly competitive broadcast news business. Philip Robenowitz, however, swiveled one-eighty in his chair and blew a smoke ring at his sloop. "Piss on ya, you British bastards," he crowed. "And piss on ya too, CNN."

"So, what did your boss have to say about all this, Miss Holly?"
Holly hesitated before answering. She knew brutal honesty might not sit well with Cappy. If the man knew the extent of cynicism in her business, he might get discouraged, do an about-face and go home. If that happened, she would lose the story and he would lose the family farm. Everything Cappy counted on hinged on her response. She took a deep breath.
"He said—he said wherever the fires of injustice rage, WNN will be there to douse the flames. We're going to help you every way we can to win back your cattle."
And, she said it all straight-faced and without one word of profanity.

The five-hour train ride from Edinburgh to King's Cross Station ran slightly behind schedule and the estimated 3:15PM arrival. Holly talked on the phone most of the way. George snored for four hours non-stop. The two cattlemen, however, remained glum and exchanged few pleasantries, preferring instead to watch the landscape skate past their window. Each man stewed preoccupied on the day's events and the prospects of Haddington Moor's future. Not until the train reached the outskirts of London did Angus began to realize that his uncle, John David Sterling, was no ordinary man. The man sitting beside him, he thought, had to be one of the last honorable human beings on earth.

"Tell me, Cappy. Is it the Texan in ya or is it something else that stirs that soul of yours?"

Cappy roused from his thoughts and raised an eyebrow. "I don't understand, Angus."

"What I mean to say, sir, is you've given up everything to help others achieve a dream. Even when the others have given up themselves, you're still there to tell 'em to keep believin'. You're there to tell 'em just how wonderful their dream is. I find that refreshing. Seems to me that since it's such strong free will, it would have to be the Texan in ya. That's all."

"Maybe it is, Angus. Who's to say? For years I listened to your aunt sing the praises of Haddington Moor. I guess her words rubbed off on me. When I laid eyes on your place for the very first time, I knew I'd made the right decision. As far as the money and the cattle—well, 'guess it's worth everything to see you and your family secure on the farm."

With that admission, Angus couldn't control his emotions any longer. He threw his arms around Cappy and smothered him in a never-ending hug. It was an unusual sight to see a fifty-year-old man tearfully embrace an aging stoic cowboy.

"I'm so sorry for behaving like I did on Saturday, Uncle Cappy. It was such a petty thing for me to do. And poor Emilio, he's such a good lad."

"There, there Angus," the older man said, patting his nephew on the back. "What you've been going through would have been tough on any man. Believe me. I know. I just about lost my ranch four years ago. We were having a really bad drought. I was losing livestock left and right. Then, Steven joined up. Put to practice some of the ideas they taught him at school and I'll be darned if we didn't turn it around. Made a heck of a profit the past two years, too. You know, Angus, we all have special God given talents in life. Maybe yours isn't cattle farming but that's okay. You have other talents just as admirable. From what I've seen, you have a rare ability for keeping family together. That's a special gift. With that sort of quality, I can't think of a better man to become the future clan thane. Now, what you need to do is take advantage of Steven's talent. Put the boy to work on the family's behalf. Let him turn Haddington Moor around. Give him the reins."

Between phone conversations, Holly overheard most of what the two men said and appreciated the tender embrace. She also realized anyone else on the train not privy to the verbal exchange, might find it all a bit odd.

"Cappy," she said, purposely butting in. "Why don't you come sit next to me? I want to go over the text of the speech I've prepared for you."

After sliding George's feet out of the aisle, Cappy scooted beside Holly. As they rehearsed the script, he couldn't help but ponder how different the day would have been had fate not steered Holly his direction. He thought her one shrewd cookie. The reporter's insight, however, could never have prepared them for the reaction to WNN's repeated broadcasts. Five hours after that initial interview in Edinburgh, other world news agencies clamored for the day's hottest story. Just who is this John David Sterling from Texas? they asked.

The taxi ride from King's Cross Station was uneventful until they turned off Whitehall onto Downing. The cab driver stopped short of their intended destination.

"Looks like there's some big to-do at the Prime Minister's residence today, Miss. This is as far as I can get you folks."

Holly thanked the man and tipped him generously. As they climbed out of the taxi, she peered toward the horde of news people milling about the Prime Minister's residence— camera crews, reporters, the armada of trucks with satellite dishes—all camped in front and blocking their way.

"Oh, crap," Holly remarked. "I should have checked to see what was happening today. Doesn't look like we'll be able to get the shoot where I'd hoped."

Suddenly, one of the journalists spotted John David Sterling, the hat being the obvious giveaway. "Look. There he is. There's the cowboy." Two hundred reporters responded to those words and lunged, surrounding the four and leaving no room for escape.

Holly managed the situation as best she could. "Get back, you maggots," she screamed. "I said, get the hell back." On that note, she began swinging her microphone by its cord bola-style with an Argentinean swagger. With each sweep of the microphone, more cord got let out, pushing the throng further back until an escape route presented itself. Taking advantage of the situation, the men climbed to the top of an adjacent stonewall. Holly got hoisted up, and the four stood precariously on the wall ledge as the mob pressed up against their position.

"Remind me, Miss Holly, to show you how to rope. You look like a natural," Cappy stated matter-of-factly.

"That's a date, cowboy," she replied. "Right now, I need to let these fools know who's in charge. By the way, that 'miracle' we talked about—look's like it's beginning to take shape."

With the floodlights and boom microphones shoved too close to their faces, Holly retaliated, firing off another barrage.

"People, listen up—listen up. I said, listen up you *f#*king* morons."

Jolted into silence, the reporters obeyed.

"*Shit,*" she mumbled. "Excuse me, everyone. I apologize for that. My name is—"

One of the British reporters interrupted. "Holly Gunter with the World News Network. Indeed. We already know who you are, Miss Gunter, and we're getting tired of hearing your name every thirty minutes on the telly. We just want access to Mr. Sterling. Quit hogging him."

Holly tried blocking out the light from the flood lamps to identify the heckler. "To whomever said that, I'll answer your comment this way: Mr. Sterling has given WNN first rights to his story. If you have questions for him, those questions are to be directed through me and I will decide which ones he will answer. Now, we're all tired, especially Mr. Sterling, so let's show him the respect he deserves before you attempt to bombard him with questions—deal?" She interpreted the silence as an affirmative. "Now, after he reads his prepared statement, we'll get to your questions." Turning to the old cowboy she whispered, "Show time, Cappy. Give 'em hell." She squeezed him on the arm for good luck.

"Good afternoon, ladies and gentlemen," he began. "My name is John David Sterling. I am seventy-eight years old and, except for when I was over here during the war flying B-17's, I've never been outside my home state of Texas—well, with the exception of Las Vegas one time."

The press responded with light laughter to his opening remark and listened attentively for the next twenty minutes, all without interruption as he spoke to them from the heart. By the time he finished, they were spellbound. Holly appeared the most impressed. Not only had Cappy flawlessly recited her script, he even managed to ad-lib the best lines without her prompting, especially the wrap-up.

"And one thing, ladies and gentlemen, I've learned through all of this is while land can be one of the most important things in a man's life, there's nothing more important than keeping your promise. You can take away land and still be a man but take away a man's word and he is nothing. With that said, I would like to close this statement of mine with a poem from my friend Robert Burns, and it goes like this:

> I'll act with Prudence as far as I'm able,
> But if Success I should never find,
> Then, come Misfortune, I bid thee welcome,
> For I'll meet thee with an undaunted mind.

Ladies and gentlemen, I believe in doing the right thing. My question to your Agriculture Minister is, does he? Whatever his answer, I still plan on facing life undaunted."

Cappy's concluding words were met with complete and utter silence. Humbled by his sincerity, no one knew quite what to say or do. Holly, however, tiptoed along the wall, kissed Cappy on the cheek, and started applauding. Another reporter joined in the applause as did another and another.

The well-dressed man in the back of the audience, however, stopped taking notes long before Cappy's finale. When the press began applauding raucously, he knew it was time to sneak away before getting spotted. Calmly, he zipped shut his black leather notebook and one-hand screwed close his Mont Blanc pen. "The Minister do the right thing?" he muttered. "Not as long as I've known him."

Here's a health to them that's away;
Here's a health to them that's away;
And what winna wish good luck to our cause,
May never good luck be failed!

Robert Burns

TEN

"Stephen, come here. *Quick.*" Heather hollered from the big house toward the stockade fencing the three cowboys were repairing. "And bring the others with you."

All three came running in trepidation, suspecting Mary Catherine had taken a turn for the worse.

"Is it Grandma?" Steven asked. "Has she passed?"

"No. *It's Cappy.* He's on the news. Look at the telly." Heather pointed to the picture on the television set.

The cowboys' jaws dropped in disbelief.

"Turn it up. Turn it up." Emilio ordered.

As they looked on, the last segment of the first interview was being broadcast:

". . .*All the way to Jesus Christ, Himself, if I have to.*"

"Looks like we're in trouble. Real trouble." Steven moaned. "What was the rest of the interview about?"

"British Customs say they won't release the cattle because of a new quarantine imposed this morning. Apparently, the reporter was right there when it got announced. They captured Cappy's run-in with an agent. They said he was heading down to London with the news crew to confront the

Prime Minister."

Steven turned to the others, upset. "I told Cappy coming here was a mistake."

"But it's not his fault," Heather responded. "He had no idea what was going to happen."

"I don't care whose fault it is. The bottom line is I'm getting screwed out of running my own operation. We should have stayed put in Texas."

"Shut up, Steven. We're all tired of listening to your negative vibes," Nate spoke out. "If you want to be the boss, start acting like one. Tough it up."

"Oh, yeah, big mouth? What would you do?"

"Tell you what I'd do. First, I wouldn't whine like a little girl every time something doesn't go my way. Other people in this family have feelings, too. Why we're here isn't just about your sorry ass—it's about family. Second, I'd go down to London and stand by Grandpa and help him kick some butt, that's what I'd do."

"Well, those are the dumbest ideas yet to come from that pea brain of yours. If we do anything, we're going to stay right here and finish mending the pens. That's what Grandpa would want us to do."

"Hey, college boy, if we don't ever get the cattle, why mess with the damned pens? We need to get our butts down to London." Nate stepped within inches of Steven, repeatedly poking him in the chest. "Understand, Aggie?"

Steven drew a fist ready to knock down his cousin. Emilio jumped between the pair, shoving Nate back. "Steven's right. We need to finish our jobs here. Cappy can take care of himself. Now, get your butt outside, Little Nate, and cool off."

Nate glared at Emilio and back at Steven, realizing he was outnumbered. He pointed his finger at Steven, "You may think you're the boss but when Grandpa gets back, I'm never taking orders from you again." He stormed out of the big house, slamming the door. Emilio chased after him while Steven and Heather looked on helplessly at the spectacle.

"Steven, I'm—I'm so sorry about all this," Heather said. "I feel horrible, especially about what I said the other day in front of Angus. If he loses this place, it'll devastate him. I don't want that and I don't want to lose you either. You don't know how much we all need you here to make this farm work."

Steven turned away to look out the window and at Emilio's attempts to pacify Little Nate. Nate was in the midst of crying with Emilio pleading to stop. The sight filled him with shame. "I've got a lot to learn about family, don't I, Heather?" he groaned. "I've been such an idiot. Please forgive me."

Heather laid her head against his back. "Steven," she whispered, "do you really think Cappy would lie? Not live up to the promises he made ya in Texas—that someday you' would run this farm?

"No. No, he would never do that. Grandpa is a man of his word."

"Aye. That he is. So, don't give up on the man. Don't lose your faith."

Steven turned around and held her tight. She kissed his cheek.

"Come on, dearest Steven. Best we tell Mary Catherine the news."

In fields they fought and laurels bought
And bulwarks strong did batter,
But still they graced our noble list
And ranked Fornicator!!!

Robert Burns

ELEVEN

After Holly fielded questions from the press, the British government issued no formal response or rebuttal. The Ministry's silence deafened all logic. Why had the Agricultural Minister not backed down? Why did his department remain so inflexible on the issue? And, why not exempt the Texas cattle from the quarantine?

The standoff provided the media the perfect opportunity to maximize coverage. Every major news organization broadcasting the event had been showing updates as quickly as they could dig up dirt on the Agriculture Department. Regardless, the most popular segments, *Captive Cattle Crisis in Scotland*, aired every half-hour on WNN and prominently featured John David Sterling, the Texas cowboy. By the end of the day, WNN had taken a commanding audience share from rival CNN. Even with the deluge of information on the event, the public demanded more coverage with an unquenchable appetite to understand what was really transpiring. By nighttime, the earlier superficial coverage had broadened into more in-depth topics such as how BSE is spread, the real risks to humans, the pro's and con's of restricting non-contaminated supplies from importation and, more importantly, why the British government hadn't declared the quarantined herd on the docks of Leith exempt from the new policy.

Yet, the hottest news topic by far was about the man who risked everything to save an ailing cattle farm in Scotland. As John David Sterling and his nephew Angus MacLaren slept soundly in their London hotel suite, the world continued to watch the newsreels and taped interviews, and fell head-over-heels in love with the cattleman from Texas. From the living rooms, sports bars, offices, and bedrooms, the world became thoroughly mesmerized. Cappy had become a media star of the first magnitude. He had become a man who stood for principle, honesty, and decency; a man who defied the odds and kept his word.

Tuesday morning got ushered in by an anonymous phone call at 5:00AM, interrupting Holly's much needed rest.

"Hello-o," she answered, still asleep and lost in a dream where she was roping cattle somewhere in Texas.

"Holly Gunter?" the mysterious voice probed.

"Yes."

"Holly Gunter with WNN?"

"Yes, that's me," she grumbled.

"I've got some information concerning Minister Sessions you might find interesting."

"Fine. Give me your best shot," she replied, still yawning.

"His family controls the bank."

"What bank?"

"The bank threatening to put the farm into receivership. It's a clear conflict of interest. Smells rotten, doesn't it?"

"Who is this?" she asked, the conversation now commanding her full attention.

"Next time, do your homework, sweet girl. Good morrow."

"Don't go," she pleaded, but it was too late. The mystery caller had already hung up.

"*Shit*," Holly cursed, slamming down the receiver. As she rehashed the mystery caller's words, it suddenly occurred to her what the leak meant. "Gotcha, you son of a bitch," she squealed, throwing back the bed covers and sprinting into the adjoining room where her cameraman lay passed out on the couch. "Wake up, George. Wake up. We've got work to do."

"What's wrong?" he asked, both eyes welded shut.

"Nothing. Everything is starting to look up. I need you to dig up some information for me. You can work with Atlanta on it."

"Damn, Holly. It's 5:00AM."

"Look, I just got a tip, a leak, and I need some things checked out and checked out fast."

"Like what for instance?"

"I need you to find out from Angus the name of the bank that holds the note on the farm. I need to find out who is on that bank's Board of Directors, who manages its daily operations, who owns the shares of stock, and what their other interests are. I need to know how many other farms they've foreclosed on in the past year and I need those locations plotted on a map. I've got a hunch about this."

"Oh, and I suppose you're going to want this today?"

"You got it, big guy. By noon."

"Why noon?"

"Because that's when I'm going to have lunch with Steven Sessions, the high and lofty Minister of Agriculture. He just doesn't know it yet."

Holly disappeared for most of the morning, doing her own research. As she had hoped, George arranged a secret off-the-record luncheon with the Minister at his exclusive Royal Knights Club in Mayfair. Upon her arrival at the club, she was unceremoniously ushered in the back door and led up a wooden staircase to the second floor and a large cathedral ceiling room stacked with musty leather bound books. A weighty set of seventeenth century double doors slammed shut behind her.

"Miss Gunter, we meet again. Welcome to the club's library." The voice echoed from a distant corner where a shadowy figure longed behind a large conference table; the man made no attempt to stand as she approached.

"Minister Sessions, I'm so glad you're here. I wasn't sure if you or one of your henchmen would actually show up. That would have been a real pity since I learned so much about you this morning. The revelations would have gone to waste."

"Well, I'm flattered you would think enough of me to ask questions, and relevant ones at that, I presume?"

"Oh, yes. Very relevant."

The Minister smiled wryly. He turned to his left. "Before we get started, Miss Gunter, let me introduce my personal assistant, Trevor Reeves. I require Trevor attend all my meetings. He has a way of keeping everyone in private meetings, like this one, honest."

Holly glanced at the tall wiry man standing in the other corner of the room. He was pale and appeared sickly. As she waved to him acknowledging his presence, he simply nodded politely, his expression remaining morose. The three of them remained the only people in the stodgy library.

"Would you care for a glass of wine?" the Minister asked.

"Why, I'd be delighted. I suppose it would have a sort of Last Supper symbolism, wouldn't it?"

The Minister chuckled nervously on the remark, attempting a comeback. "Does that mean you're getting ready to crucify me, Miss Gunter?"

She brushed aside the question and sat down, smiling all the while. "I propose a toast," she offered, teetering on the front of her chair. "Here's to John David Sterling: May he always triumph over adversity."

"I'll drink to that," the Minister responded, attempting to maintain his composure. "I have nothing against the old gentleman."

"Oh? So I guess you've seen him on the news?"

"Well, I would be lying if I said I had not. Our government's catching a lot of—how would you Yanks phrase it—a lot of *shit* on this incident. Yes, I do believe that is the colorful colloquialism from the Colonies. Right, Trevor?"

Trevor said nothing. He simply nodded his head in agreement.

"Miss Gunter," the Minister continued, "just why did you request this meeting?"

"Because I wanted to be with you when you get exposed for the slime you really are."

"Oh? Explain what you mean by that."

"It's quite simple. I came here because I wanted to see the expression on your face when the world learns the truth about you and your kind. I want to watch you squirm. Like when your balls are in a vise and someone's turning the handle ever-so-slowly and putting on the squeeze." Her hands gestured as though she were actually turning a handle and loving every second of the torture.

"Ah-h-h. And what makes you think I'll squirm for you?"

"Because I've got you by the balls, *Stevey* boy."

"Miss Gunter, I'm a busy man. It's obvious you are both impudent and ill mannered. Come to the point."

"All right. Here it is, *Stevey*." She grinned, quite pleased with herself. "The bank that holds the MacLaren's past due note, the bank that's ready to foreclose on the farm, is none other than the Bank of Tyne Waters—*your family's bank.*"

"That's all well and good, Miss Gunter, but if you did your due diligence you would have also discovered how once I became a minister in Her Majesty's government, I was forced to put my controlling interests into a blind trust. Thus, I'm no longer directly involved with the bank."

"Is that so? Well, since your departure from the board of directors, you've *indirectly* replaced a majority of its members with family. The same family who jointly own Lowlands Oil and Exploration with your trust."

"And what does that have to do with anything?" he pressed.

"Well, in the past twelve months, coincident with your government's demands of cattle exterminations and, I'm guessing, the motivation behind this quarantine, the very acts of which are driving the farmers into bankruptcy, Lowlands Oil and Exploration has bought up the foreclosed parcels that your bank has conveniently taken over. At a very reasonable price, I might add. You see, *Stevey*, the way I look at it, your ministry's policies are purposely driving the cattle farmers out of business so your bank can sell the land to your oil company. And, here's the best part." She looked to her right to make sure Trevor was listening before lowering her voice, "the word on the street is there's a newly discovered deep crude field in the Lothian valley near North Berwick, centered at White Castle Fortress—or am I just naively fresh off the cattle boat?"

The smirk vanished. Minister Sessions hastily gulped the remains of his wine. He stared at Holly without showing any emotion and applauded. "Bravo. Well done, Miss Gunter. You're a clever girl, aren't you?"

"My big brothers didn't raise a fool, *Stevey*." She scooted back in her chair and appeared relieved. "I'm going to really enjoy watching your resignation speech. Maybe even the Prime Minister's, too."

The minister stared at his empty glass, lost in thought. His mouth puckered as though he had swallowed a bitter pill. A few seconds later, however, the smug expression reappeared and he sat up straight pouring himself another glass of wine.

"You do realize that you can't have it both ways, Miss Gunter?" he asked, more as a statement.

"What do you mean?"

"I mean, the way I look at it is you can go ahead and release your in-depth investigative exposé and I'm sure it will force a vote of confidence. I am sure that I will be forced to resign in disgrace and there will be years of litigation ultimately ending in some sort of compromise between the overpaid solicitors representing the people and those representing the Sessions' estate. But, you will never get the one thing I think you really want."

"And what's that?"

"The gentleman's cattle released before the bank deadline."

Holly's eyes spooked. Before she could respond, Sessions continued his rant.

"He'll lose it all. By the time the courts settle the matter, he'll be long dead and buried and I'll be living on some Caribbean island immune to lawsuits, fat and filthy rich. So, what is it going to be, my dear Miss Gunter? My head, and perhaps the downfall of this government, or the much needed cattle for Haddington Moor?"

"You're telling me if I keep my mouth shut—"

"If you keep your mouth shut, you little twit, he'll have access to his herd by noon tomorrow. It will take us that long for final inspection, approval and stamping. As I recollect, the bank deadline is midnight tomorrow. That gives him twelve hours to truck his precious cattle the measly thirty mile distance."

Holly grimaced. "Why, you mother *fuc*—"

"A-a-ah-ah. No need for that sort of language in the club," he broke in. "Actually, I've been called far worse names, even by Mother." The minister moved in closer to Holly, scooting his chair forward with his chest pressed against the edge of the table. He peered deep into Holly's eyes. "So, once again, which is it going to be—my head or the old man's cattle? Your call."

Holly almost leaped over the table. An armistice had never been part of the battle plan yet, if she exposed the Minister as a corrupt politician, Haddington Moor farm would be lost forever. Until the cattle grazed safely on its moors, she was powerless to wage war. The cagey minister had astutely read her vulnerability—John David Sterling.

So may thoughts filled Holly's head: How much longer could the other farmers endure the minister's deceitful self-serving policies? How much longer could the British government support a corrupt politician who placed family wealth above true public interest? She hated his kind and everything he stood for. Still, she could not abandon Cappy. She could not retreat from what she initially set out to do— free up the cattle. Wrestling with these sentiments, Holly capitulated. Her adversary, Steven Sessions, had won.

"All right. I'll keep my mouth shut if you'll release the cattle by noon tomorrow after the final inspection. You've got a deal." Her voice quivered with the word 'deal.' As she extended her hand to seal the agreement with a handshake, he quickly seized hold and shook it, grasping it far longer than necessary.

"Deal," he said. "Just remember, releasing the cattle by noon won't necessarily bail out your cowboy."

"Oh, no? And, why not?"

"Because he's still got to prove to the bank the land is supporting an on-going cattle operation. Therefore, the herd needs to be in place no later than midnight. From what I've heard, there's not a single head of steer at Haddington Moor. Bank rules mandate at least one head per two acres or there can be no loan extension. That rule has to be enforced. No exceptions. It's been the common banking practice in Scotland for years and has nothing to do with me or my family's oil investments."

"With over five hundred head on the docks, satisfying that rule shouldn't be a problem. Right?"

The Agriculture Minister didn't reply. Instead, he motioned for his assistant to escort the reporter back down the staircase. Hurriedly shoved out of the library, Holly babbled all the while, pressing for an answer to her question. A minute later, she was standing on a street curb wondering who got the best of whom. Meanwhile, her escort was doing his best to hail down a cab.

"Trevor, how can you stand to work for that man?"

"Well, sweet girl, it does have its moments," Trevor stated straight-faced, adding, "and, I do sincerely wish your cowboy friend all the success in the world. He seems so innocent in this jaded world of ours."

A taxi screeched to an abrupt stop and Trevor held the door open while Holly climbed inside. As he bent down to assist her, his Mont Blanc pen fell out of a shirt pocket. She picked it up off the taxi's floor and handed it back to him. He thanked her, politely, saluting her, and shut the door. Holly never heard his farewell as the cab sped away.

"Good morrow to you, Miss. *Good morrow*."

In proving foresight may be in vain;
The best laid schemes of mice and men,
Gang aft agely,
And leave us naught but grief and pain,
For promised joy!

Robert Burns

TWELVE

They had narrowly escaped the paparazzi and reporters pursuing them once they fled from the hotel. Holly explained to Cappy that if he took off the cowboy hat he would be less recognizable. He informed her that in spite of his newly acquired celebrity status, his hat was one of the last vestiges of Texas—he'd as soon be penned up with the cattle as separated from the hat. Given all they had been through, Holly politely bowed out of the discussion, and avoided an argument. She also tactfully never informed him of her lunch with the esteemed minister. In fact, nobody knew. All the public and press knew was how at 3:00PM an unknown spokesperson for the Agriculture Ministry announced that the quarantined cattle at the piers of Leith would be cleared by Customs the next day, after a final inspection; the cattle had earned a rare government "exemption." Bottom line: the MacLaren family had won and was now free to take possession of the livestock after Cappy's documents received Her Majesty's formal stamping. Upon hearing the good news, Cappy shook Holly's hand and thanked her without gloating in their triumph. Angus, on the other hand, kissed Holly full on the mouth and danced a jig up and down the hallway of the hotel.

Understandably, Holly was quite pleased with herself and the difference WNN had made. She had forced Minister Sessions to back down. She had also catapulted her news organization into the ratings lead with a full four-point gain. In fact, Philip told her the ratings were so good that he had put in for a September retirement. Would she care to go sailing with him? he asked. "Yes," she answered and, shortly thereafter, made airline reservations for Boca.

Thus, with her job now complete, Holly snuck Cappy and Angus back on the afternoon express returning to Edinburgh, and parted ways with the two cattlemen. As the train conductor processed their tickets, he did a double take, disappeared for a few minutes to process other passengers, and returned to chat.

"You're the gentlemen the news has been covering, aren't you?"

"Yes, we are," Angus beamed. "I'm Angus MacLaren and this world famous celebrity to my right is my uncle, John David Sterling of Texas."

"Honored to make your acquaintances," the conductor replied excitedly, shaking their hands. "My name is Clarence Oxford. Friends call me 'Ox.' The Missus and I watched the news last night and felt rather badly for the two of ya. She tried all morning to call a complaint into the Ministry Office but never could get through. All the lines were busy. Sounds like others were upset as well. I guess it all turned out for the best in the end. Congratulations on kickin' their Tory rumps."

"Thank you kindly, Ox. We appreciate your show of support," Cappy responded.

"It just didn't seem right to me, Mr. Sterling. I mean, with you sacrificing so much to help us out over here, what they were doin' just stunk to high heaven. So, how's your wife doing, sir?"

"Well, last night when I called, they wouldn't let me speak to her. The doctor was in the room. She'd been sedated and put on some medicine that's supposed to ease her discomfort. She's a real fighter but barely hanging by a thread. I just hope I get there before she passes. I want to be by her side in her final hours."

"You don't need to say anything more, sir. I know exactly what you mean. It's a good thing you caught this train when you did or ya would have been stranded in London for sure."

"And why's that?"

"The strike, man—the national transportation strike." The conductor paused with the bewilderment showing on Cappy's face. "I thought you knew, sir. Everything gets shut down at midnight. This is the last train to Edinburgh. You made it just in time. I guess someone was smiling over your shoulders."

"Hold on there, Ox. You mean everything transportation-wise gets shut down tomorrow, including trucks?"

"Yes sir. That's how these things work over here. Everyone is in the union and union members strike in solidarity. It's not like in America. So, if you are concerned about your cattle, don't be. I'm sure this thing will blow over soon enough. Won't last more than two or three days and—"

"*Two or three days?*" Cappy squealed. "We don't have two or three days. Our deadline is tomorrow at midnight or the bank takes possession of the farm." Cappy turned to Angus, visibly upset. "Angus, who do we need to talk to at the bank to get an extension until the strike is over?"

Angus shrugged. "I don't think they're gonna grant us one, Cappy. They've already extended our deadline twice. They told me there would be no third time, at least without cattle on the land. They even had a notary serve me formal papers saying as much. 'Can't recall the bank officer's name."

"Damn it all, Angus," Cappy screamed, losing all composure with the outburst. "Now think. Who was the bank representative?"

"I don't remember, Uncle Cappy. It's been so long. We went into receivership even before the cattle got put down. It's been almost a year."

"A year? This happened *before* you exterminated the cattle? A whole year before? Why didn't you tell us?"

"Because—because I couldn't. I couldn't bear for the family to know I was responsible for losing their birthright. I was ashamed to admit I didn't know how to manage the business."

"So, what you're telling me is that other than the money I wired you, the bank hasn't been paid anything for a full year?"

"The bank never got paid any of the money you wired. It all went to pay off taxes and feed the family. I thought for sure we would have the cattle by now. I was thinking they couldn't seize the place once we had your Texas herd grazing on the land. That we could negotiate a new loan and, and—" Angus stopped. Tears streamed down his face. "I've really buggered this up, haven't I, Uncle?"

Cappy closed his eyes in disgust. The revelation blindsided him. With the truth finally exposed, he realized everything sacrificed had been in vain. He slumped forward on the train seat, buried his head in his hands and began rambling incoherently, "My God, what did I get us into? We risked everything on this move—*everything*. We should have stayed put in Texas. Oh, Lord, what have I done? Oh, Daddy. Dear, Daddy. I am so sorry for selling Rancho Rio Concho. I am so, so sorry. . . . What to do now? What to do?" He fell to his knees and clasped his hands in prayer. "Oh, Lord, please help us through this horrible ordeal. You can fix this mess. I know You can. If You want, You can do anything to me. Punish me here and now. Just make it right for the others—for Miss Mary and the family. Just help us get through this rough patch. And, if You've got anything left to give, Lord, please help me, too. Help me persevere—*persevere?*" He paused after saying the word and mulled over what the meaning of it had meant throughout his life. "That's it," he whispered. "Perseverance." He remembered how his father had instilled the word in him. Perseverance was the key to surviving those harsh dust bowl days at the ranch and escaping poverty and hunger. Perseverance was the inspiration to never give up or capitulate even when life appeared bleakest.

When Cappy lifted his head, Angus was rocking back in a grief-like stupor. Poor Angus, he thought. Running a cattle business had exceeded the man's capabilities since day one. His poor nephew never told anyone about the problems; he never turned to anyone for direction. Cappy's heart poured out to the man and the anguish being felt.

"Nephew, we all make mistakes," he said softly. "I just wish you had been honest with all of us. Your aunt and I risked everything on this move, but we will survive this obstacle. We will get through this thing. We are MacLarens and Sterlings. We can overcome anything together if we just persevere, can't we?"

"Aye. I suppose we have no choice on the matter, Uncle. We can overcome anything if we want it badly enough. If we're willing to fight for it."

"That's the spirit. Now, let's put our heads together. Here's what we need to find out: Who runs our bank?"

"I think his name is Rich or Richard—yes. *Yes.* It's Richard Sessions. That's it. Maybe he'll listen."

"Well, I'm not supposed to do this," Ox remarked. "But why don't ya call him from my cellular phone? I've got a private compartment you can use where no one can hear your conversation."

Cappy placed his hand on Angus' shoulder. "I'm sorry I yelled at you, Nephew. I had no right to do that. Just do your level best and get us that extension."

"I'll try but I've heard he's a scoundrel of a businessman."

"Just give it your best shot," Cappy encouraged. "If that doesn't work, we'll figure out something else."

It was 9:00PM when the two men reached Waverley Station in Edinburgh. They took a taxi to the location where they parked the Defender the day before. Despite his pleadings, Angus had not been successful in persuading the bank president, Richard Sessions, to grant them a loan extension on the deadline. The sly executive officer had stated repeatedly that an extension was not impossible without at least one steer per two acres of land *or* a government stamp on the customs papers that showed the livestock pre-approved for release, a catch-22 of sorts. Should the Sterlings be able to fulfill either of those stipulations before midnight, the next day, the bank's loan committee would grant an extension "by necessity."

Cappy had also called Holly for help. She promised to be there first thing in the morning to assist the family. She made it clear to him that this newest battle would not be as easily won. Banks, she said, had a different agenda than governments; banks would not as easily intimidate or embarrass. And, with the Bank of Tyne Water waiting over a year to foreclose, it showed both "restraint and prudence" by the institution's management. Still, she knew Minister Sessions had double-crossed her by relying on both the transportation strike to do his dirty work and centuries old banking laws to enforce the possession. "The most important thing," she told Cappy, "is to stay cool, calm and collected. Whatever you do, don't do anything rash. Wait until I get there."

In spite of her words, Cappy remained anything but clearheaded and calm. When he and Angus returned to Old Rover, he politely excused himself. "There's something I need to do before we leave. Can you wait here?" he asked. "It'll only take about thirty minutes."

"No problem, Uncle Cappy. Go do what ya have to do. I'll be waiting for ya in the pub next door. By the time you get back, I'm sure I'll be drunk. I'm in a strong drinkin' mood."

Cappy walked across the street and slipped through the Customs House pier gate and back to the compound where the cattle quarantined. He knew every day the livestock remained in the government's custody was another day of expensive feed he would be billed—money he did not have. As he searched through the lots, he finally found the pen housing Ben. He greeted the longhorn with the remnants of a last cookie that had been crushed and reduced to crumbs by a day and a half on the run.

"How ya doin', old boy?" he asked, gently stroking Ben on the head and inspecting the Ben's ears. "No ticks. Looks like they've been doing a good job keeping you clean. Shoot, this isn't such a bad place after all, now is it?"

Ben said nothing in response. He did snort, however, and kick the stockade sharply with a hind leg.

"By that I guess you're telling me you want out of there. Well, there's nothing I'd like better, Ben, but the truth of the matter is I don't know when I'll be back to get you. You see, if we get evicted from Haddington Moor tomorrow, I won't even have a place to graze you. My guess is the bank will come to pick you up right away. As far as they're concerned, you're just another asset to sell off to help pay the debt. So, we're kind of in a pickle, aren't we?"

Ben blinked woefully while continuing to sniff Cappy's hands for another cookie. Today the longhorn's kingdom could be bought with a single ginger snap and the brief companionship provided by his two-legged friend. Tomorrow he would dream of endless green pastures and ripe young heifers, and remain oblivious to the swirl caused by greedy humans.

When Cappy finished talking, he turned around and faced the other bulls and the heifers, and the lone calf. He looked at them all and swallowed hard, afraid he might actually lose his 'children' due to no fault of his own. The intimate bond formed over years would simply vanish with the stroke of an auctioneer's gavel. "I'm so sorry, boys and girls," he whimpered, bolting out of the compound sobbing. "I guess I failed you."

As promised, thirty minutes later Cappy rejoined Angus at the tavern across from the Customs House.

"Angus, I thought you said you were going to get drunk? You look pretty sober to me."

"Thought better on it, Uncle. Only had one dram and the barkeeper, here, even announced the drinks were on him."

"Is that so?" Cappy asked, turning to face the man standing behind the counter. "That's awfully nice of you, son."

"Oh, think nothing of it, sir," the man replied. "We all know who ya are, Mr. Sterling. We've seen ya in the newspaper and on television. You're a regular hero around these parts. Everyone knows how important the cattle are to auld Scotia and how hard you've been fighting those nasty Brits."

"Well, I appreciate the positive words but with this transportation strike, it looks like our goose is cooked. The bank has us right where they want us. What makes it so darn frustrating is we only need to have our papers stamped. Without trucks to ship our cattle, the cattle can't get released. Without the cattle getting released, customs won't stamp our papers. Period." He turned to look past the window and to the docks across the street. "It's all a nightmare. A bureaucrat nightmare. Why, our livestock is within spitting distance and I'm powerless to do anything."

The bartender sensed Cappy had given up. He reached across the counter and squeezed him on the shoulder. "Mr. Sterling, if I may be so bold as to speak my thoughts on this dilemma."

"Go ahead, son."

"Well, sir, we have a saying in our clan that I think can help ya in this wee bit of a jam ya find yerself in. Goes like this: If the brain had all the answers, there would be no need for God. I suggest ya simply go with your instincts, sir. Put your faith in God and in your heart. They'll always lead you to the right place. After all, you are a cowboy. Do what comes natural to cowboying," he added with a wink.

Cappy looked into the young man's face. There was something familiar about it. Then, he remembered. He remembered his aviator friend from the war, Robert Duffy, who often repeated the same saying.

Perhaps, it was at that moment when inspiration struck. For in that brief instant, an idea occurred to Cappy—a wonderfully bold and enlightened idea.

"Thank you, son. Your clan is absolutely correct. Years ago, I did that very thing. I let my heart dictate a decision and I ended up marrying the most wonderful person in the world. A month ago, I put my faith in moving everything here to Scotland. I know in my heart that also was the right thing to do, too. So, yes, I do know now what I have to do. Like you said, I am a cowboy." Cappy turned and grabbed Angus by the shirtsleeve and tugged his nephew out of the pub to the curbside and Old Rover. "We have a lot of work to do, Angus," he said, opening Angus' car door. "A lot of work. Get in."

As Old Rover sped away from the curb, the sun's evening rays lit up the sign above the tavern door, the sign inscribed with the words 'Duffy's Pub.'

By my ill requited;
By the faith you fondly plighted;
By the pangs of Lovers slighted;
Do not, do not leave me so!
Do not, do not leave me so!

Robert Burns

THIRTEEN

"Ya can't do it. I'm tellin' ya, Cappy, they'll stop ya from using the public roads and right-of-way," Angus argued.

"Look, you said it was exactly twenty-nine point five miles. I know we can drive the herd that distance in way less than twenty-four hours and get 'em to Haddington Moor by sunset."

"But the police will stop ya."

"Heck, Angus, look at these roads. Nobody's driving 'em now and it's 10:00 at night. By midnight there won't be a soul out. We'll take the herd right through the city, down the main thoroughfare to the town of Haddington. We just need to get 'em over the bridge that spans Tyne River by noon. Then, we're home free."

"But Cappy, the authorities—when ya hit the rush hour traffic they'll be out to nab ya."

"First, we'll be going against the grain. Second, by that time of morning, we should be at least eight miles from the docks and beyond most of the suburbs. Besides, Angus, how are they going to stop five hundred stampeding head of cattle?"

Angus's eyes opened wider as he pondered the sight. A sinister smile swept over his face. "This idea of yours, Cappy, is starting to agree with me. Scotland has never seen the likes of a cattle drive, let alone with real cowboys at the lead. It should be one heck of a sight."

"That it should, Nephew. And, the way I look at it, it's our only real chance. Now, I want you to repeat back to me what your job is while we're driving the herd."

"That's easy. I'm going to implement our *Plan A*. I'll be at the bank the minute its doors open in the morning. I'll approach Mr. Richard Sessions and tell him that his presence is required at Haddington Moor by sunset so he can witness the cattle grazing on our property, thereby fulfilling the loan extension requirement."

"And if he refuses?"

"That's when I go to our *Plan B*. I take the shotgun out from underneath me jacket and I shove it up his rump, telling him either he's goin' peacefully to Haddington Moor or he'll make my day."

"Well, I don't know about the Clint Eastwood stuff, but those are the game plans, all right. I suggest you lure him outside before you try to kidnap him. Just don't take the gun in the bank for Pete's sake. That way no one will know he's actually being kidnapped or where to look for him. Oh, and don't forget the duct tape."

"Aye, those are the plans," Angus assured. "Just one more question, Uncle?"

"What's that?"

"Do ya have a spare cowboy hat for the future thane of Haddington Moor?"

"For you, Nephew, you betcha."

The two men remained silent the rest of the way home. Cappy memorized the route and retraced the last leg twice along the back roads. By the time they drove into the farm, the last of the sun's rays peeked beyond the horizon from the northwest.

The long summer days worked to their advantage. Cappy determined that with Scotland so far north, he would have over eighteen hours of daylight to drive the herd. The risky part of the trek would be the first five hours with the cattle shrouded in complete darkness. Angus assured him that if he stuck to the main thoroughfare, he would have streetlights to guide him, at least to the suburban town of Tranent. After Tranent the sunrise would be directly in their faces—that is, if everything went according to plan.

Once they reached Haddington Moor and parked the car, Cappy asked Angus to assemble the family in the big house. First, he needed to visit Miss Mary in the bothy.

Heather and Elizabeth had been keeping Mary Catherine company. Pedo sprawled on the bed by his mistress's side. Mary Catherine had been unable to retain food for nearly two days and was extremely weak from the ordeal. Her skin had turned leathery and slightly yellow from the onset of jaundice and the first signs of kidney and liver failure. Most terminally ill patients with the disease would not have survived this long. Mary Catherine had simply willed herself to live so she could see Cappy one last time. Even so, Mary Catherine lay half-asleep and half in a drug induced coma. Cappy barely recognized her and was shocked by her rapid deterioration.

After the two women left the room, he knelt by the bed and held her hand. It was cold and trembling. He kissed it gently and held it to his cheek. He knew life without her would be void of any meaning, a thought that caused him to break out in a panic. How would he survive after her passing? he wondered, grimacing in pain. He had tried to avoid the question for nearly two months. Selling the ranch and moving their belongings to Scotland had preoccupied all his spare moments. What would he do now without her by his side? He reached over to stroke the dog's head and noticed a new bandanna around its neck. Pedo proudly adorned in the tartan colors of the MacLaren clan. Cappy smiled. Pedo's tail wagged furiously.

"You're a good boy," Cappy whispered.

The words stirred Mary Catherine. She blinked, slowly opened her eyes and gazed upon her husband. Even her joy to see him could not hide the capitulation to the illness. If he could just keep her alive for one more day—just one more day, he thought.

"Cappy, is that you?"

"Yes, sweet wife."

"I was just dreaming about us. Mother and Father were in the dream, too. We were all on my hill overlooking Haddington Moor. And, we were drinking shots of tequila out of Mother's demitasse cups, and she liked our little tradition. *She approved of it.* It was a grand dream, Cappy," Mary Catherine stated in a whisper, straining to be heard. She took a deep breath before continuing, "I knew you'd come back. The girls told me you were on television. They said you wrestled the cattle from the government. I knew you could do it. You're a man of your word. Aye, that you are."

Cappy's eyes began to tear. He had hoped he could keep from crying in her presence. He clearly did not want to lose his emotions with so much at stake, but it was proving impossible. The two of them simply had too many years together for him not to feel heartache. As he capitulated to the feelings, he began to sob openly while she continued to hold his hand.

"Miss Mary," he muttered, "we're not out of the woods. I'm afraid there's a transportation strike bogging us down with no way of getting the cattle home except to take 'em back from the government. His words failed to evoke a response. Maybe she didn't understand, he thought. "What I'm saying is we're going to have to mount an illegal cattle drive tonight out of Edinburgh. It's our only chance and it's risky. Tomorrow is the bank deadline. So I guess—I can't be here with you."

"That's all right, Cappy," Mary Catherine assured. "You need to be with the boys. You are their leader. Go do the thing and take Pedo with ya. It's not a cattle drive without him along. Make me proud of you all."

"But, I want to be here with you, for you. If you were to leave me so, I—I don't think I could handle it."

"I'll be here when ya come back, Cappy. Do ya really think I'd miss my cowboys bringin' home the cattle?" she asked, already knowing the answer.

"You'll hold on until I get back?"

"I'll hold on.," she said. "*I promise.*"

He kissed her and they embraced.

"Just hold on until sunset, Mary Catherine," he whispered. "You have my word I'll be here by sunset."

"Grandpa, we're all here," Steven announced, the first to speak up at the hastily assembled family meeting. "Angus filled us in on the transportation strike and we all feel the sooner we get started, the better. And, sir, we're all with you one hundred percent."

"Thank you, Steven. I appreciate it."

Steven continued. "While you were with Grandma, we talked amongst ourselves and this is what we came up with: First, we know we're going to need to get the cattle off the main highway as quickly as possible, so we'll have to get them moved out no later than an hour from now. Second, we're bringing a couple of crowbars and flashlights to break into the shipping crate where the saddles and gear are kept. We're not real sure what kind of shape the horses will be in but just getting them out of those pens and on a run beats what they've been going through the past four weeks. And third, to get past the security gate we're probably going to have to overpower the guard. Angus said he'd help out in that department."

Cappy looked around the room at everyone. Angus was sporting the cowboy hat he asked for earlier and a new pair of sunglasses.

"That's right, Cappy," Angus interjected. "The guard either opens the gate or it's <u>hasta la vista, baby</u>."

Cappy shook his head. "What do the rest of you think about this plan?"

"What choice do we have, Cappy?" Emilio asked, as though the answer quite evident. "If the bank has already given us an ultimatum, it'd be too much of a risk to depend solely on their mercy, after the fact. I say we do it."

"Me, too, Grandpa. Let's go kick some butt," Little Nate threw out.

"But Cappy, don't you think the authorities will do their best to stop ya once the herd is on the main thoroughfare?" Elizabeth asked.

"I'm sure once they realize what's happening, they will. But, it'll also be long after sunrise before they figure anything out and, by then, we'll have our trump card ready."

"And what's that?" she pursued.

"WNN." He grinned.

"Cappy, in answer to your first question, we've all talked about it and agree that this thing needs to be done. Our prayers will be with you the entire way," James stated.

Heather spoke up. "Katy and I were saving these as a surprise for you men. We think now's the time to give 'em to ya."

As Heather spoke, Katy handed each man a green, red and gold bandanna made from the same tartan cloth adorning Pedo's neck.

"We just couldn't imagine having cowboys at Haddington

Moor not wearing the clan's colors. We want you to wear the neckerchiefs on this cattle drive of yours to bring you good luck," Heather explained.

"Aye, and when you drive the beasts home, we'll have the entire clan waiting for ya, bagpipes and all," Katy added. As she spoke, she adorned Nate's neck with the tartan bandanna and kissed him on the cheek.

"Well, people, I guess there's only one more thing for us to do," Steven said, winking to Nate. "Gather in here and stack your hands on top of mine."

The family formed a tight circle with their hands interlaced in the center, one upon the other.

"Whose land does this belong to?" Steven asked, pointing to the ground.

"That's our land," the cowboys responded in unison.

"Man-oh-man, I see the hands and I hear the voices, but I don't feel the spirit," Steven preached, admonishing the non-participants. "Now, whose land does Haddington Moor belong to?"

"That's our land," they cheered together.

"Louder so Grandma can hear."

"THAT'S OUR LAND."

"Louder. . . ."

For our sincere, though haply weak endeavors,
With grateful pride, we owe you many favors;
And how so ever our tongues may not reveal it,
Believe our glowing bosoms truly feel it.

Robert Burns

FOURTEEN

"Who goes there?"

"It's John David Sterling and his ranch hands. We're here to inspect our livestock."

"Are you the same gentlemen that was with Mary Catherine MacLaren?" the man asked, peering through a misty fog at the shadowy figures.

"Yup. One and the same," Cappy responded, now recognizing the familiar voice.

"Good evenin' to ya, sir. It's me, Little Robbie—I mean, Robert, Robert MacAllister. I met you folks the other day when you came off the ship and passed through here," he continued, unlocking the gate as he spoke. "I've been watchin' you on the news and said to meself, 'that Mary Catherine sure found herself one special man,' if you don't mind me sayin' so, sir. You saved the old place. Good for you."

"Thank you, Robert. You're too kind, but the farm hasn't been saved, at least just yet. The MacLaren clan needs your help."

"Oh, no? What can I do? Just name it, sir."

"Well, for starters, I need this gate kept open and unlocked for another twenty minutes. Then, I need you to look the other way."

"Look the other way from what, sir?"

"The five hundred cattle we're going to be taking out tonight."

"Well, where are your trucks? You do know there's a strike goin' on?"

"There won't be any trucks, Robbie. We're taking the herd cowboy-style."

"Through the streets, sir? Without final inspection? And without your papers being stamped? I don't think so."

Cappy motioned for the others to precede past the guard shack to the cattle pens. The security guard watched as the three cowboys strutted by as if unaffected by his presence. From the glare of a distant streetlight, his eyes strained to catch a glimpse of their silhouettes. All three men sported wide-brimmed Stetsons. Green plaid bandannas smartly wrapped their necks. Leather chaps hugged their blue jeans; and, weathered cowboy boots with spurs welded to the heels broke the still of night. The spurs clanged with each synchronous trod of their gait until the sound disappeared into the misty fog. Only Cappy and Angus stayed behind. Robert became suspiciously nervous.

"I know the herd's exempt from this dastardly quarantine, but if you don't have your paperwork stamped, I'm afraid I can't let you take the cattle." He eyed both men, thought for a few seconds on the impasse, and gradually began to smile furtively, giving them a wink. "*But*, if you were, say, to overpower me and tie me up, anything is possible, isn't it, gentlemen?"

Angus laughed and shook the guard's hand. "You're a good fellow, Robbie MacAllister. I knew we could count on ya. We owe you a big favor." Cappy also shook Robbie's hand and thanked him before darting off to join the others.

Angus seated the elderly guard in an office chair and bound the man with duct tape. "You know, Robbie, I heard this tape has a million and one uses. I guess it now has a million and two." Angus giggled.

Robbie nodded in agreement since the tape plastered tightly over his mouth.

The crate containing the bridles, saddles, ropes, and riding gear pried open and within minutes all of the cowboys had saddled and mounted their horses. Ben got led out of the compound first. Next, the pen gates were thrown open one by one with Pedo began barking orders at the Brangus in the back to move forward. The startled bulls obeyed and positioned themselves behind Ben. The heifers followed the bulls. Cappy and his two grandsons brought up the rear while Emilio pulled up behind Ben. Up to this point, no one had uttered a word. Even the Brangus remained hush as though they understood how silence played an essential ingredient to the breakout. Once the last of the cattle were in the open, Cappy waved to Emilio, signaling to him to begin the drive. The ever-confident Tejano flipped the tail of his whip behind his horse and, with the flick of the wrist, cracked it inches above Ben's head. The longhorn turned around backward and stared stubbornly at the lead cowboy, refusing to yield to the threat of a whip. A long slobbery snort ensued.

From the rear, Cappy hollered, "He doesn't like the whip. Just whistle and tell him to head 'em out."

Emilio shook his head, disgusted over Ben's preferential treatment. "All right you prima donna stubborn spoiled carcass of good-for-nothing cowhide—*Head 'em out.*" He whistled, frightening the other five hundred cattle (but not Ben).

Sensing urgency, Ben decided it best to move toward the cobblestone road spied in the distance and the orange vapor streetlight glowing like a beacon. He slow-trotted past the open security gate and the two well-wishers in the guard shack. The rest of the herd followed Ben's lead.

"*Aye-aye-aye*. Head 'em out. Move 'em on, cowboys," Cappy yelled.

The rest of the cowboys responded with whistles and shouts, pushing the herd at a hurried pace to follow the lead established by Ben and Emilio. The entire contingent exited left out of Customs House and stampeded in an orderly procession past Duffy's Pub. In less than a minute, the herd had rounded the first corner and out of sight of the guard shack. Only the sounds of the hoofs beating the cobblestone roadbed broke the midnight still.

"Well, Robbie, that's a sight you'll never see again, I'll bet, 'less you care to join the clan this evening at Haddington Moor when they bring 'em home," Angus remarked.

The guard nodded he would be there. Nothing could keep him away, not even the exhaustive inquisition from superiors he would face later that day.

Once underway on the divided motorway, Cappy and Emilio switched places since Cappy knew the route. Five minutes later, not a single auto passed them. Meanwhile, a steady fog blew in from the Firth of Forth inlet running parallel to the road. The fog shrouded the herd from sight and added to what would become a flawless start.

"Dang, if this don't beat all. No traffic. No people. No nothin'. 'Eh, cousin?" Little Nate remarked as he rode beside Steven. Nate swept his flashlight in a three-sixty circle without spotting anything on the move except cattle. "This town is deader than a doorknob."

"I think luck has something to do with it," Steven replied. "We just need to hope this fog holds up." Steven turned around and peered through the haze on their flank. "Nate, you take up the rear and keep that flashlight aimed away from our backside. I don't want anyone ramming us."

"You got it, boss man," Nate replied, backing up his horse, twirling and galloping away.

"Emilio, how ya doing over there?" Steven shouted.

"Easiest drive I've ever been on. Have you ever seen the cattle so well behaved? It's like they know something's up."

"Yup. I think Grandpa's been talking to 'em again. Looks like they listened this time."

As the two hollered over the clatter of the hoofs, Pedo roamed from side to side, spurring the strays back in line. Occasionally, a heifer would tear loose and the aggressive cattle dog would charge, nipping the vagrant's flanks and forcing it back into the tightly packed herd.

Fifteen minutes into the drive, the first auto approached from the rear with a young couple behind the wheel. They slowed to a crawl when they saw the blinking flashlight. The young man driving the car rolled down his window and cautiously pulled alongside the cowboy on horseback. Fog swirled around Nate and with orange vapor lights casting a glow over his shoulders, the driver could scarcely believe the ghostlike apparition.

"Either I've had too much to drink this evening or you're an American cowboy driving cattle through the streets of Edinburgh," the man remarked.

"They're the cowboys that's been on the news, you lout," his date piped, slapping him on the arm as though he should have already known. She crawled over the driver's lap, poking her head out the window to gaze at Nate. "Hello there, handsome."

"Howdy, Ma'am," Nate replied, tipping his hat.

"Need any help?"

"Yes, Ma'am. With all this fog, I'm afraid someone might slam into our herd. If you've got flashers for your tail-lights, if you could just turn them on, That'd probably make this, here, cattle drive a heck of a lot safer."

The woman turned to her date. "Freddie, turn your emergency flashers on." She repositioned herself back out the side window and continued jabbering. "So, tell me, cowboy. Where are you taking your cattle so late at night? I grew up on a farm and I know the police don't give permission to block the roads, so I hope for your sake it's not much farther."

"Hate to tell you this, Ma'am, but we're driving 'em about eight miles southwest of Haddington."

"Oh, goodness. You're going to have your hands full. Tell you what. I know something about cattle. Freddie and I'll take up the rear so you can stay up with the others. With this many head I know you're needed elsewhere."

"But your mother gave me a curfew," Freddie interjected.

"Shut up, Freddie. Mummy will understand—*I hope*," she replied, pondering the consequences after breaking the rules once or twice before.

"That's awfully kind of you, Ma'am," Nate said before galloping away to help Steven and Emilio.

Twenty minutes later, four more cars had caught up with the herd but the young couple intercepted them all. Once the other drivers had been told what was happening, three of them decided to stay and help. Forming a wall four cars abreast, all with flashers flashing, they systematically blocked any potential rear-end collision. Angered by the blockade, the fifth driver exited for the nearest constable's station.

As the night progressed, the cowboys adjusted to their environment and the cards nature had dealt them in the early morning hours. They learned to take advantage of the center embankment separating the divergent traffic lanes and use the guardrails like a funnel to keep the cattle pushing forward. Nate drove the herd from the rear, but only on an as-needed basis. Emilio, Steven, and Pedo kept the stragglers from drifting beyond the shoulder and into the ditches. Cappy covered the left-front flank with Ben.

Early on, Emilio relayed the message to Cappy how local citizens were assisting in the undertaking and protecting their flank. Cappy felt greatly relieved by the gesture. When he devised the plan, he worried how motorists would react to traffic delays caused by the slow gait of the cattle. He knew a favorable public response could make or break the drive. Yet, being the focus of a television blitz, Cappy had no idea what a positive spin the media created, nor how enthusiastic public sentiment would be to lend a hand. It was a sentiment not shared by the local police.

Sixty minutes and a mile and a half into the drive, the first squad car tore past Cappy and slid through a grassy ditch, almost spinning out of control before speeding farther ahead. Seizing a strategic position a hundred yards in front, the vehicle deliberately skidded sideways and slammed on its brakes. Meanwhile, its red and blue lights bounced off the fog in a kaleidoscope of colors, spooking the cattle. Ben bawled in displeasure at the blinding sight but Cappy soothed the longhorn with his reassuring voice. "It's okay, Ben. We just need to keep moving. Stick with me, old boy. Stick with me." Cappy never saw the two constables step outside their squad car, before one of them began barking through a bullhorn.

"STOP AT ONCE. THIS IS THE EDINBURGH POLICE. WE ARE ORDERING YOU TO HALT YOUR CATTLE, IMMEDIATELY. STOP AT ONCE."

The warning accomplished nothing. Cappy continued moving the procession onward, quickening the pace as the herd drew nearer. Fifty yards from the squad car, Cappy could make out the expressions of the two officers as they sensed the futility of their one-car blockade. When there was less than twenty yards to spare, the two men jumped back inside. The driver slammed the door shut and rolled up his window. Cappy chuckled hysterically at the sight, knowing the two officers had made a wise decision. Seconds later, cattle swirled about the squad car and rocked it back and forth as the animals' hindquarters crushed up tight against the bumpers.

"We're lucky to have escaped alive, Willie," the driver gasped. "Best we call for backup."

"Why, Jonathan?" Willie replied. "By the time backup arrives, they'll be out of our jurisdiction, anyway. I say we let the East Lothian Chief handle it. That one is a real bastard. He'll take care of those unruly Yanks for sure."

At first, the East Lothian Chief Constable's office ignored the radio plea for assistance and considered the request a practical joke. Once the officers convinced the dispatcher they were on the level, it took another thirty minutes to locate the on-call deputy who was being secretly entertained by a married woman in North Berwick. Fortunately, luck and ineptitude favored the cowboys. Even by 4:00AM, after the fog began to lift and the first peek of blue shone on the horizon, the cattle drive was proceeding on schedule and on an unstoppable pace.

"You've done this before, Little Nate?" the woman asked. Her date, the driver, did his best to ignore her overt fascination for the young cowboy.

"Don't I look like the kind of drover that's done this before?" Nate grinned. "But, I gotta confess, I've never driven 'em at night. Guess we're breaking new ground," he replied, periodically whistling at a stray.

"What's it like bein' a cowboy in command of those huge dumb steer from the backside of a magnificent horse?"

Nate thought for a moment how best to answer her, and abruptly swiveled around to face her. "Well, why don't you climb out that window and join me? You can find out what it's like firsthand."

The young woman ordered Freddie to pull closer to Nate's horse. Even before she finished wriggling herself half out of the car, Nate grabbed her by the waist and hoisted her up on his lap.

"Oh, my. That was quick, wasn't it?" she masked as a question.

"I'm known for quickness. Now, what's your name, darling?"

"Ann."

"Well, Ann, today's your lucky day. You get to see what driving a herd cowboy-style is all about, and from one heck of a fine Texas cowboy, I might add."

"Oh, my," she cooed. "Just feelin' how you take command of the situation, I do believe that you are."

Nate conveniently wrapped his arms around her while she handled the reins. For the rest of the night the weight of two riders burdened his horse. Freddie tried dismissing the sight of his girlfriend with another man as "nothing" and, instead, focused on his assigned task. In reality, he stewed more preoccupied by how Ann's mother would react at 5:00AM than by the amorous advances of the brash cowboy.

Coming through the rye, poor body,
Coming through the rye,
She was draggin. . . .
Coming through the rye.

Robert Burns

FIFTEEN

Holly's hastily assembled plan called for taking the eastern highway marked on the map as route A1. The road hugged the coast north from Newcastle and traveled quicker than the interior expressway. With no buses or trains running, traffic out of London clogged bumper-to-bumper along the normal arteries. Once the WNN news crew passed Northampton, however, the bottlenecks disappeared and they made good time. By 5:30AM, they had skirted passed the town of Haddington and easily beat the rush hour traffic into Edinburgh. Avoiding the beltway, they followed the thoroughfare leading directly to the docks. Their goal was the Customs House where Holly planned to conduct a live interview with Cappy in hopes of regaining public support for his latest predicament.

In spite of her much ballyhooed plans, Holly had no idea Cappy stole his cattle hours earlier from under the nose of the port customs authority. Now, just past the outer Edinburgh loop, she noticed flashing blue lights and what appeared to be four or five police cars approaching from the oncoming lanes.

"George, wake up. *Wake up*."

"Huh? What now, Holly? I drove all night, for Pete's sake."

"Something weird is taking place up ahead. Stick your head out and let me know what you see."

George rolled down his window. Cool morning air flooded inside, sending shivers down everyone's back. Positioning his upper body out and above the roofline, he peered toward the opposite lanes, squinting to keep the wind from his eyes.

"I see a bunch of squad cars in the far ditch. They look like they're tailing some old timer on a horse. The old timer is leading a bunch of cattle. Hey, what are cattle doing on the motorway? *Shit*. Holly, that old-timer is Cappy."

Holly slammed on the brakes and almost got rear-ended from the rubbernecker behind; the inertia carried George halfway out the window. She spun the car around and drove across the shoulder to the access road.

"What in the world are you doing?" George screamed.

Holly didn't hear a word George uttered. She accelerated to the overpass they whizzed by moments earlier.

"I can't believe he did it, George. I had a hunch he would do something crazy like this, the old fool. He just couldn't wait for me. *No-o-o-o*, he had to do it on his own. He didn't trust Holly, did he?"

She raced the car to the overpass and swung back in the opposite direction, on the other side of the road, breaching the far ditch and spinning the car, yet once again, into a wild one-eighty tailspin stop. George, fortunately, had hunkered down and fastened his seat belt. The two waited as the herd moved to their position. Meanwhile, the squad cars in pursuit of Cappy and his cattle appeared ready to pounce.

"George, I want this captured on the camera. Look at those idiots trying to arrest him. They don't have a clue about the fight they're about to get into. Not a *f#*king* clue."

With their car now stationary, George repositioned himself back through the window, facing backward with his elbows on the roof and hands clasping the camera. Holly rolled down her window and accelerated slightly so the lead cowboy and herd could pass them. By so doing, she also hoped to cut off the contingent of pursuing squad cars.

"Cappy, just what are you doing?" she yelled above the wailing sirens.

"Morning, Miss Holly," he replied, a tad too casually. "What's it look like I'm doing?"

"I know exactly what you're doing, Cappy. You'll never get away with it."

"Oh, really? Well, these fine young deputies told me their boss grew up on a farm. He gave them instructions to escort the herd all the way to the town of Haddington. And compliments of the Chief Constable of East Lothian. What do you have to say about that?"

Holly couldn't believe it. She remained skeptical. "I'd say you are one lucky cowboy, you old coot. Why, if you were just forty years younger."

"Give me the benefit of the doubt, Miss Holly. How about twenty years younger?"

She wanted to laugh aloud but had to pay attention to her driving to avoid sideswiping guardrails. "Does WNN still have first rights?" she asked.

"Heck, yes, but the officers, here, told me some other news crews are on their way up here, so you'd better start filming fast if you want to be the first."

"I've got to hand it to you, Cappy. You've already figured out how to play the press."

She grabbed her microphone and one-hand steered the car parallel to the drive's heading. George pulled himself back inside the vehicle and focused the camera on Holly with Cappy leading the herd in the background.

"This is Holly Gunter with late-breaking news on the

daring cattle rescue by Texas rancher John David Sterling. Just when he thought he had won the battle, he discovered he was losing the war, a war pitting the family farm against an uncompromising bank deadline. . . ."

The cattle drive reached the town of Haddington by 2:30 that afternoon. As they pushed toward the village center and prepared to cross Waterloo Bridge, Cappy let out a long overdue sigh. With the worst parts behind, the back roads beyond Haddington would provide a much-needed sanctuary from the traffic and pursuing camera trucks that had been dogging the drive the previous eight hours. The ongoing press coverage fostered an unofficial hands-off policy from the local authorities along the route. The coverage also perked an unprecedented public following.

Beyond Haddington, the countryside provided more latitude to graze and water the herd free of human distractions. Cappy's five hundred and one children had exceeded everyone's expectations. Through it all, the livestock seemed to possess a sixth sense about the importance of the situation.

As the drive turned west toward the river, Cappy spied up head what he assumed at first to be an ambush in the middle of the town. He held up his hand and shouted to Ben, slowing the herd's momentum to a crawl. In the distance, lining the way to Waterloo Bridge and on both sides of the road, nearly two thousand well-wishers had assembled. To get to the crossing meant the herd had to pass an enthusiastic mob of parade-happy citizens. Sometime earlier in the day, the town councilmen of Haddington declared the event a holiday; the townspeople responded full force to cheer on the cowboys, Lothian style, and wave British and American flags along a hastily prepared but well orchestrated route. Cappy even thought he heard bagpipers straining to play *The Eyes of Texas*, all without much success.

As they drew closer, an unrestrained cheer arose from the fans. Someone unfurled a hanging banner draped across the street. Cappy squinted to read what it said: WE LOVE OUR COWBOYS. He smiled at the sight and politely tipped his Stetson to the crowd. He liked this town, he told himself. He liked it a lot. In appreciation of the crowd's hospitality, he heel-squeezed his palomino's flanks, re-positioning it to face the people square-on, and pulled up the reins. His horse reared obediently, jabbing its front hoofs in the air. With perfect timing, Cappy raised his hat high above his head and waved to the well-wishers. They responded with a rousing cheer.

Emilio galloped to his leader's side to see what was causing the slowdown. "What in the world is happening up there, Cappy?" he asked.

"Well, son, we must have friends in high places. Looks like the entire town came out for a parade and *we're it*. I don't want to disappoint the townsfolk, but we're going to need to drive the herd down the street as quickly as we can so the bulls don't spook or go on the attack."

With that, Cappy shouted an order to pick up the pace. The wranglers responded by spurring the herd faster along the narrow parade route with the bridge the objective. The crowd applauded as the procession streaked by. Shouts of "Give 'em hell cowboys" and "Scotland loves you, lads" competed with the clatter of hoofs and cowboy whistles. Even with the distractions, the bulls held together and pushed in tight along the cobblestone route leading to the Tyne River.

Little Nate abandoned Ann just as they entered Haddington, freeing him to kiss babies and young mothers (one of the advantages of being in the rear guard). There was little need for him to do much else with the cattle following Ben and Cappy like obedient soldiers.

The camera crews captured the enthusiastic welcome

from the ground and overhead. Swooping from the direction of the river, helicopters hovered above the town's rooftops while jockeying the congested skyway. One of the helicopters, however, did not have the distinctive markings of television call letters on its tail. Painted a dull khaki green, its camera operator wore army style fatigues.

Less than a mile beyond the bridge, where the road curved and disappeared into a rare thicket of trees, a man dressed in a stylish Armani suit monitored the event for his own private viewing. One of the SWAT officers interrupted him to confirm the sighting.

"Sir, they'll be here any minute."

The man turned off the television set and groaned as he screwed close his Mont Blanc pen. "Well, I guess we have to follow our instructions, don't we, officer? Do you have the service papers prepared?"

"Yes, sir. I'll serve them personally."

"Good. I don't have the stomach for it."

With the town of Haddington behind them and after successfully crossing Waterloo Bridge, the drovers easily reached the Garvald turnoff and the bend in the road in a matter of minutes. Lulled into a short-lived euphoria, not one of the Texans suspected the British Customs Department had taken a stand so close to Haddington Moor. Cappy spotted the four semi-trucks first; the trucks jackknifed to head off the herd and block the road. Eighty helmeted agents in full riot gear lined up before the trucks, armed and ready to seize the livestock and take the herd by force if necessary. In unison, they beat their Kevlar shields with nightsticks in a deafening cadence while striking a ready to attack pose. The sound spooked the steers.

Cappy healed his palomino, cautiously sidestepping the horse closer to the agents. If only he had followed the rules, he told himself, none of this would be happening. But, he also knew that bureaucratic formalities such as stamping release papers were clearly out of the question, given the transportation strike and the looming bank deadline. Either way, it appeared clear that the British government never intended for his cattle to reach the farm.

To Cappy's right and left stood formidable barriers—the walls and rock hedges crisscrossing the countryside. To the rear, the news crews' massive broadcast trucks blocked any hope for retreat. The only way out lay between the trucks.

The wind suddenly picked up. Dust from the roadbed swirled about and cloaked the cowboys and their cattle. Cappy swatted the debris from his face and tried focusing on the idea of stampeding the herd past the agents and between the semi-trucks. *Yes*, he thought. That is exactly what they would do. The timing was right. He would signal the charge and—

A voice blared over the PA system mounted atop the command vehicle.

"MR. STERLING: WE HAVE A CEASE AND DESIST ORDER FROM HER MAJESTY'S GOVERNMENT. YOU ARE TO IMMEDIATELY SURRENDER ALL LIVESTOCK IN YOUR POSSESSION. THE AGENT APPROACHING YOU CARRIES SERVICE PAPERS DEMANDING YOUR ORDERLY RETURN TO THE EDINBURG CUSTOMS PORT."

Cappy halted the herd less than a hundred yards from the trucks. Steven, Emilio, Holly and George, and Pedo raced to his side.

"Looks like they've finally caught up with us, Grandpa. Never thought it would be out here, and so close to home," Steven confessed.

"Cappy, let 'em have the cattle," Holly interjected. "It's not worth a pitched battle. Someone could get hurt. I still have a few tricks up my sleeve. I know how to fix this."

As Holly continued pleading, a SWAT officer approached

on foot with his arm extended, holding the service papers. When the agent neared to within a few feet, a loud crack of a whip pierced the uneasy standoff. The papers immediately vaporized; fragmented pieces scattered in the wind.

"If I were you, mister, I'd keep away, especially if you're carrying government orders," Emilio warned, coiling up the whip's tail to use it a second time.

The agent screamed in terror and retreated toward the command vehicle. Meanwhile, a second unidentified stranger approached on foot, this time from the rear.

"Excuse me. Excuse me, Mr. Sterling. My name is Henry Bodine. I own the farm on the other side of this rock wall. My land runs for a mile along this road and up the same direction you're headed." With his introduction out of the way, the man inched closer, feeling more confident. He continued, "I didn't know if you knew this, sir, but they can't take your cattle if the cattle are on private property. Under any circumstance. That's the law. Bank or no bank. That's the way it's been for nearly three hundred years in Scotland. It's one of the concessions we got from the Brits when we signed the Act of Union in 1707. And, sir, you've got my permission to run your cattle through my private fields. My neighbor and his neighbors have also agreed to let you drive 'em through their fields as well." He paused to study the confusion in Cappy's eyes. "What I'm saying, Mr. Sterling, is that we've all joined together and opened our fields for ya, all the way to Haddington Moor farm. *And, there's not a damned thing the government can do about it, neither.* That is, sir, if you care to give it a go?"

Meanwhile, George's camera captured the entire event live. "Man, this is going to win you a Pulitzer, Holly," he kept whispering.

Holly spouted, "Let's just get the man's cattle home."

Cappy jockeyed his horse around to look at the stranger face-to-face. "I appreciate your generous offer, Mr. Bodine."

"Well, sir, what you're doing for all of us here makes us better people. You're standing up for cattlemen everywhere and we're deeply indebted to you and your family. There's just one problem, however."

"And what's that, Mr. Bodine?"

"The rock hedges and fence rows are goin' to be a real obstacle to the cattle and you've still got at least seven more miles to go."

"To hell with obstacles," Nate yelled, galloping to the front. "Mister, we have a genuine jumping longhorn with us and nothing, I repeat, nothing is beyond what that bull can do." He turned to the cattle dog. "Pedo. Make Big Ben jump that rock fence," he commanded, pointing at the wall.

Without a hint of hesitation, the blue heeler strutted to Ben, looked the bull in the eyes and yelped two or three times. The bull refused to budge. Instead, it cocked its head sideways and stared at Cappy for instructions.

"Ben, old boy. This is that miracle we talked about," Cappy said softly. "Now, go do it. Go jump that wall—do it for Miss Mary."

It was after his coaxing that Cappy thought he heard his friend say something to the effect of, *"Anything for Miss Mary."*

The longhorn spun toward the wall, drug its front hoofs twice against the rutted pavement, snorted, and charged full speed, leaping over the rock hedge and knocking down the top row of stones. By so doing, an entire swath of the wall collapsed, breaching a tumbled rock-strewn opening for the others to follow. Five hundred Brangus and heifers leaped for freedom.

"Well, you boys know what to do now, don't you." Cappy hollered with the widest toothiest grin he had mustered in days.

"Heck, yeah, Grandpa. Been there. Done that," Little Nate declared. With those words, Nate's horse reared and easily jumped over the remains of the wall with Nate shouting out, "*E-e-e Ha-a-a-a*," and chasing after Ben and the cattle.

The other horsemen followed their brash cousin's lead, whistling and yelling, "*Yip, Yip, Eye-o-o-o. E-e-e Ha-a-a-a.*"

George and Holly hoisted the calf over the barrier.

Meanwhile, Cappy twirled his steed in a tight circle as the agents came charging. He shouted as they drew nearer, "Remember this all of you: <u>A cowboy always keeps his word</u>." Then, Cappy spurred the flanks of his palomino. His horse leaped the wall and galloped off in the distance. The customs agents stopped short of the rock barrier, powerless to pursue.

"Did you film all of that?" Holly asked her cameraman.

"Yeah. I got it but I still don't believe it," George answered.

Trevor Reeves watched the event from inside the command vehicle. He, too, smiled for the first time in a long, long while. "God speed your journey, sir," he whispered. "God speed."

The sun had already begun to set when the clan assembled outside the bothy to face the rye-laden hill known as Drum Ridge. The family surrounded Mary Catherine who was propped up in a makeshift bed so she could watch her men bring home the cattle. The bagpipers primed their leather satchels with all the wind and energy they could gather. The violinists practiced their melodic wail with their bows rosined and ready. The cousins sported their most formal kilts and clan garb while guest of honor, banker Richard Sessions, got seated prominently in front and secured with duct tape to an uncomfortable ladder-back chair. Angus and Robbie MacAllister sat astride to the man, guarding their prisoner's every twitch.

Helicopter crews continued to broadcast the cattle drive as the herd stampeded across the open rolling moors of the

Lothian valley. A worldwide television audience numbering over a billion watched in awe. As the family waited on the highly anticipated arrival, they, too, glued to the television set that was moved outside for the event. Katy spoke first.

"Look everyone, the telly is showing 'em crossing Fen Burn. They'll be a heading over the ridge any time now."

Less than a minute later and directly in line with the setting sun, a deafening rumble broke the calm.

"My God, it sounds like an earthquake." Heather exclaimed.

"Aye, that it is," whispered Mary Catherine. "One made by man and beast. They're bringin' home the cattle, dear Heather. They're bringin' home the cattle."

As the clan peered toward the horizon, a magnificent longhorn charged forward. The bull stopped to bow at the spot where Mary Catherine once picked her twinflowers on the crest of Drum Ridge. It dragged its front hoof twice across the meadow's crest, carving the ground in a royal gesture. Satisfied this new land was now home, Ben charged full speed toward the pens spied in the distance. Behind the lead bull came the rest of the herd in full pursuit. Dust kicked up by the stampeding livestock exploded skyward. An approving roar from the family echoed across the glen. Now fully cued, the bagpipers and violinists began their music welcoming the drovers to Haddington Moor. As the beasts raced across the meadow, the men on their horses followed, spurring the herd on with shouts and whistles as their cowboy hats flailed the air. The sun radiated behind the four horsemen and lit up their silhouettes in white brilliance as though the four ignited in fire. Watching their approach, Mary Catherine's eyes welled with tears.

"They look so much like angels to me," she whispered.

Through all the commotion, no one heard her words, for the clan was lost in the moment and in the sights and sounds of the hurried procession.

As the cowboys neared the bothy, Cappy broke rank from the others and galloped full speed toward the awaiting family, furiously swatting his horse's neck with the reins. Watching her cowboy approach, Mary Catherine waved to him from afar. When he saw she was still alive, he skidded to a halt and pulled up on the reins. The palomino reared on its hind legs. Cappy stood tall in the saddle with his hat waving triumphantly overhead and called out to his wife, "You're looking beautiful as ever, Miss Mary."

She whispered one last time before closing her eyes, "I so love you, too, Cappy." she said. "I so love you, too."

A Last Promise

As day was dawning in the sky,
We drank a health to bonnie Mary.
                                        Robert Burns

SIXTEEN

By the time Cappy reached Mary Catherine's side, she had already fallen into a coma from which there would be no awakening. Only days before, she asked to be buried in her secret place as the sun dawned on a new day, and so it was that the family complied with her last wish. The cousins carried the casket, which draped in the family's tartan colors, up the steep hillside. From below in the valley, the braying and bawling of cattle played sweetly to the procession's ears. The two grandsons walked beside their grandfather. Steven's arm interlocked with Heather's arm, while Emilio led the group. As they climbed to the lookout spot, Little Nate asked his grandfather if it was true that he and Emilio were returning to Texas.

"Yes, I'm afraid it is. We're going back on the same boat that brought us here," Cappy replied. "You see, Emilio's in love and as for me—I just miss Texas too darn much. Frankly, I'm getting too old for all of this."

Little Nate suddenly felt lost without his grandfather's guidance and steady presence. "Will I ever see you again?" he pressed.

"Sure you will. I'll be back—*I promise.*"

"But—"

"You have my word on it, Little Nate."

"But what's going to happen to us without you?"

"Well, judging from the looks of things," Cappy answered, peeking over Nate's shoulder at Steven and Heather, "I'd say you two men will do just fine."

"I know Steven will be okay, Grandpa, but how bout *me*? What should I do?"

"You? That's easy. Listen to God and follow your heart, Nathaniel. Do that and you'll always be led to the right place. Trust me."

After the service, Cappy asked the three cowboys to stay. When everyone else had left, he removed four demitasse cups from his coat pockets. From behind an adjacent grassy knoll, he took out a black Hussong tequila bottle stashed the night before. Pouring the cowboys a cup full of tequila, he turned to address them for one last time.

"Years ago this family started a tradition, a tradition I now pass on to you three today. That tradition, simply put, is when you boldly defy the odds, when you defy life, itself, and can squarely look it in the eye and say, 'I am the master of my own fate,' you celebrate the occasion with praise. The four of us accomplished what some would have said was impossible. We defied the odds and this family is better for it. I am so very proud of every one of you. You are men of your word. So today, in keeping my promise to your grandmother, I again toast her with praise, just like I did the very first time over fifty years ago—Gentlemen, raise your glasses on high."

And, Cappy cleared his throat to recite the poem committed to memory:

"Go fetch to me a pint of wine,
and fill it in a *demitasse*;
That I may drink before I go,
a service to my bonnie lassie;
The boat rocks at the Pier of Leith,
full loud the wind blows from the ferry,
The ship rides by the Berwick Law,
that I may—may. . . . *leave* my bonnie Mary.

Gentlemen: To Texas, Scotland, and Miss Mary."

In unison, the cowboys responded: *"TO TEXAS, SCOTLAND, AND MISS MARY."*

EPILOGUE

(*2012*)

Yesterday was the sixteenth anniversary of Grandmother's passing. To honor the occasion, my daughter, Little Mary, and I climbed the steep hill that buttresses the secret lookout at Haddington Moor and cradles Grandmother's gravesite. We struggled for what seemed like hours to reach the summit and pay our respects. As we approached the crest, my daughter, being full of pent-up energy, ran ahead. Winded by the ordeal, I stopped to soak up the aromas of the heather and rye grass and gather my breath. For the moment, I was content to watch roadrunners chase each other in the fields and to recall those fond memories from years before. By the time I did manage to catch up to Little Mary, she had already laid flowers by the headstone.

"So, she really liked these wild pink twinflowers, Daddy?" she asked, turning to watch my approach.

"With all her heart and soul," I answered.

Mary smiled with my response, pleased her flower selection had been so perfect. Suddenly, she became quite serious and closed her eyes to say a silent prayer. After she finished and stood, I noticed one twinflower still clutched in her hands.

"And just what are you going to do with that one?" I asked.

Mary did not hesitate. "Why, I'm going to give it to him," she replied, laying the flower next to my grandfather's headstone. "He needs pretty flowers, too. Right, Daddy?"

"Yes," I said, hoisting her in my arms and hugging her for

fear of ever letting go. "He needs pretty flowers, too—Know why?" I asked.

"No," she responded, shaking her head.

"Because he once told me to follow my heart and it would lead me to the right place—and it did. It led me to you and Mummy and Haddington Moor," I stated, kissing her softly on the cheek. "Now, let's go find your Uncle Steven and ride those wild ponies."

"Can we really? *Really?*" she pressed.

"Of course, we can," I answered. "Would I lie to you?"

"No, Daddy. A cowboy always keeps his word," she stated while pressing her hand flat against her heart. "A promise is a promise."

"That's right," I said. "That's exactly right."

Other books by David Martin Anderson. . . .

The Last Good Horse

Four-Bagger

John From

Harry's Apology

(all available in paperback and e-reader)

Made in the USA
Charleston, SC
13 April 2012